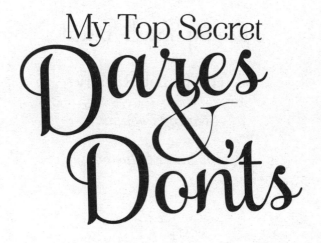

My Top Secret
Dares
&
Don'ts

Also by Trudi Trueit

Secrets of a Lab Rat series

Stealing Popular

The Sister Solution

My Top Secret

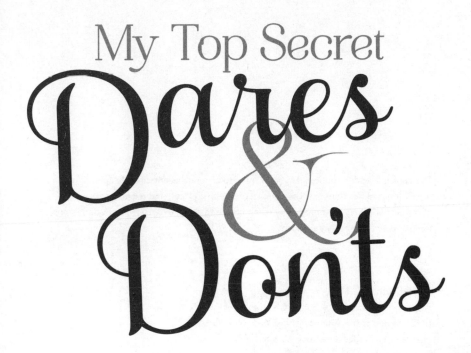

Dares & Don'ts

TRUDI TRUEIT

ALADDIN

New York   London   Toronto   Sydney   New Delhi

This book is a work of fiction. Any references to historical events, real people, or real places are used fictitiously. Other names, characters, places, and events are products of the author's imagination, and any resemblance to actual events or places or persons, living or dead, is entirely coincidental.

ALADDIN

An imprint of Simon & Schuster Children's Publishing Division

1230 Avenue of the Americas, New York, New York 10020

First Aladdin hardcover edition March 2017

Text copyright © 2017 by Trudi Trueit

Jacket illustration copyright © 2017 by Eda Kaban

Also available in an Aladdin M!X paperback edition.

All rights reserved, including the right of reproduction in whole or in part in any form.

ALADDIN and related logo are registered trademarks of Simon & Schuster, Inc.

For information about special discounts for bulk purchases, please contact Simon & Schuster Special Sales at 1-866-506-1949 or business@simonandschuster.com.

The Simon & Schuster Speakers Bureau can bring authors to your live event. For more information or to book an event contact the Simon & Schuster Speakers Bureau at 1-866-248-3049 or visit our website at www.simonspeakers.com.

Jacket designed by Laura Lyn DiSiena and Greg Stadnyk

Interior designed by Laura Lyn DiSiena

The text of this book was set in Adobe Garamond Pro.

Manufactured in the United States of America 0217 FFG

10 9 8 7 6 5 4 3 2 1

Library of Congress Control Number 2016962758

ISBN 978-1-4814-6905-0 (hc)

ISBN 978-1-4814-6904-3 (pbk)

ISBN 978-1-4814-6906-7 (eBook)

For my dad, with love

Fear cannot kill you. It just makes you think it can.

1

Dare to Be Truthful

*H*ow's the trip going?

My left eyeball is throbbing in rhythm to my little brother's kicks on the back of my car seat, the breakfast burrito I had an hour ago is churning up a tornado in my stomach, and I'm less than one hundred feet from leaving the only country I've ever called home.

Greater than great! I text back to my best friend, Langley, and regret it the instant I tap the mail button.

Dang! And I just put that on my Dares List too: *Dare to be truthful.* It's a habit of mine—keeping lists. I don't know why I do it. Langley read an article that said people make lists so they can feel as if they are in control of their lives. I'm not sure about that. I don't feel very in control of my life at all. My two most important lists are my Dares (things I want to do) and my Don'ts (things I don't want to do). Once in a while, something from the Dares List gets moved to the Don'ts List, like the time my mom talked me into trying lutefisk (I was daring to try new foods). It's pronounced "lewd-a-fisk." Lewd is a good description for it. It's codfish and it tastes like gooey soap. That's all you need to know. Once in a while (but far more rarely), something from the Don'ts List gets moved to the Dares List, like when I said I would *never* grow out my bangs. I figured I was being too rigid on that one, because never is well, never. I *did* like my longer hair, once I got through that awkward sheepdog phase. Growing out bangs is the ultimate endurance test. Nobody knows about my Dares and Don'ts lists, not even Langley. You gotta have a few secrets, right?

"We're almost there," says my mom, drumming the

steering wheel. It's the third time she's said that in the past ten minutes. Looks like I'm not the only one who is having trouble being honest today.

I hang my achy head out the window. I count six cars between the yellow posts and us, which means I am going to hear my mom say that sentence at least three more times before we cross the border. For late June, which is usually cool and cloudy in the Northwest, it's a humid day. The thick, dewy air smells like freshly mowed grass with a hint of cow—a big cow. The sky is a white sheet of haze, as if the clouds are too depressed to create even the simplest swish pattern. I can relate. Resting my cheek on the top of the door, I line up my right eyeball with the yellow post on my side of the car. Once we pass it, there will be no turning back.

I am trying to keep it together. I don't want to go to Canada. Worse, I feel terrible about not wanting to go. When your grandfather dies, you're supposed to drop everything and rush to your grandmother's side to help. I *do* want to help, but I *don't* want to drop everything. I am the most selfish granddaughter on the planet.

My mother is talking again. "... so if the customs officer asks you a direct question, answer it but don't say too much. And don't say too little, either. And Wyatt, no wisecracks."

My brother grunts. He is eight. The kid grunts at everything.

Mom taps my knee. "Please sit up, Kestrel. We don't want to give them any reason to be suspicious."

I picture a team of border patrol officers racing toward me, guns drawn. One of them flings open my door. *Out of the car!* he shouts, fighting to keep a snarling Doberman from lunging at my throat. *We don't let slouchers into Canada.*

I giggle at that, but my mom's head pivots, so I quickly straighten my lips, as well as my body. I don't want to argue with her. We still have a long way to go. It's 215 miles from Seattle to Whistler, and we're not even halfway there.

"Uh-oh." My mom slaps her hands across the dashboard then flips the lid on the utility box between us. She starts pawing through it. "Oh, no! No, no, *no!*"

"Forget something?" I ask.

She is throwing things on my lap: a pad of sticky notes, her phone charger, a bottle of hand sanitizer. "If I don't have it—"

"What?"

"The consent letter. I can't take you into Canada without a letter from your dad, because he isn't riding up with us. That's the law. This is a nightmare. What am I going to do? I can't believe I forgot it—"

"Mom." I clamp my left hand on hers before she can toss the garage door opener at me. With my right hand, I pop the glove compartment latch. Resting on top of our birth certificates and passports is a folded piece of paper. I lift the edge to show her Dad's signature. "See? You gave it to me to put with everything else."

She lets out a big breath. "That's right. Thanks."

"Mom, get a grip." I snap the glove compartment shut then begin putting all the stuff in my lap back in the utility box. "Why are you so nervous, anyway? It's not like we're criminals or something."

"I can't help it. I think it started in Mrs. Allard's PE class in seventh grade. She was a real taskmaster. You couldn't have even one shoelace longer than the other or she'd take off points. Now, any time I have to pass inspection, I sort of—"

"Freak out?"

She winces. "Yeah. Sorry."

I get that. Last year, Mr. Ruddameyer, my math teacher, could scare the fingernail polish off me. He'd get irritated when we—I—didn't understand what he was trying to teach. I'm glad they don't make you calculate the area of a trapezoid to get into Canada. I'd be rejected, for sure.

I pat my mother's shoulder. "Try to keep it together, Mom, so they don't think you're kidnapping us, okay?"

That gets a slight grin from her. "I'll try, Little Bird. "

That's my family's nickname for me. Kestrels are birds—falcons, actually. Only one type of kestrel lives in North and South America, the American kestrel. It's the smallest of all the raptors. May dad likes to say, "Kestrels may be mini, but they're mighty." He's right. They *are* great hunters, but since I'm also short for my age I know he's saying it to encourage me.

My phone chimes. It's Langley again.

Are you in the mountains yet?

I let my thumbs fly. Not even close. We're in Lynden still waiting to cross. My mom is fruiting out. I miss you already.

That's better. *Dare to be truthful.*

Same here times a million, comes the reply. Annabeth is here. She says hi!

Say Hi back!

The throbbing moves from my head to my heart. My two best friends are on summer vacation without me. This wasn't how it was supposed to go. You only get one summer before seventh grade, and Langley Derringer, Annabeth Kim, and I had ours completely mapped out. We were going to paddle Langley's canoe around Lake Wilderness and eat s'mores. We were going to sleep over at each other's houses and make homemade ham, pineapple, and olive pizza. We were going to hang out at the mall and eat frozen yogurt (we always get three different flavors and switch after every three spoonfuls). We were going to do everything and nothing, but we were going to do it *together*. And with food. However, only a few days into summer break, my grandpa Keith died. He had a stroke. It hit me pretty hard. I cried for a few days. Considering I hardly knew my grandfather, I guess it didn't make sense to Langley or Annabeth why I was so upset. Maybe that's why. I *wanted* to know him. A granddaughter should know her grandparents, don't you think? I don't know mine, though. I talk to Grandma Lark and Grandpa Keith briefly on the phone at Christmas and on my birthdays. We chat about basic stuff like school and sports (I do cross-country and soccer), but that's it.

Mom says we went to see my grandparents in Canada a few times when I was a baby and they visited Seattle once. I was four when they came. I don't remember much about it, except for one day—the day Mom, Dad, Grandma, Grandpa, and I went to the Space Needle. The second I saw the yellow capsule-like elevator inching up the side of the hourglass-shaped structure, I wanted nothing to do with it. I tried to pull away from my dad. Grandpa Keith knelt down. He held out a large, strong hand and showed me a gold ring with the biggest, reddest ruby I'd ever seen. He said it was a magical ring that put an invisible shield of protection around him and if I held his hand the magic would protect me, too. "I promise you'll be safe, Little Bird," he'd said. "And you should know I *never* break a promise." Something in the way he looked at me told me I could trust him. I put my hand into his, my fingers practically disappearing in his giant palm. Grandpa Keith didn't squeeze my fingers the way adults do when they want you to know who's in charge. He let *me* do the holding. And he kept his word. Nothing bad happened. Still, to this day, I don't like heights.

"We're almost there," says my mother again.

I watch a navy MINI Cooper peel off from the front of the line. It putters up the hill past a faded, red A-frame restaurant with green trim. The sign on the front says RUN FOR THE BORDER CAFÉ. Beyond the café is a fenced pasture with several horses grazing in the tall grass, their dark brown coats glistening in the morning sun.

I don't know how long Mom, Wyatt, and I will be gone. Nobody is saying, but I'm keeping my fingers crossed it's no more than a couple of weeks. I wish Dad would have come, too. After all, Grandpa Keith is—was—his father. When I asked Mom why Dad wasn't coming with us, she said what she always says, "He can't get away right now. I'm sure he'll have more time—"

"—after the trial," I finished for her. My dad is an attorney. He practices environmental law. Mom always says, and I quote, "He'll have more time after his current court case finishes." He never does.

"Grandpa Keith didn't want a memorial service, otherwise your dad would have come," my mother said. "I'm sure he'll get up to visit us on a weekend—"

"—after the trial," I said again.

I have another text. It's a selfie. Langley and Annabeth are cheek to cheek with wide smiles. Annabeth is taking the picture. Langley is holding a homemade sign that says WE ♥ U KESTREL! The heart is made out of pink glitter glue. Awwwww! I start to type back, but tears blur my vision. It takes me a few minutes to blink them away. Sniffing, I write ♥ U 2!

"We're almost there," says my mom.

This time, she's right! We *are* almost there. There's only

one car between us and the redbrick building with the border guards: a black Hummer. I flip down the sun visor to check my face in the mirror. I have good skin. So far. No pimples yet, though Annabeth says they are coming, says they started exploding onto her face one day like dozens of miniature volcanoes. I wipe away a smudge of mascara on my eyelid. I am allowed to wear mascara and lip gloss, as long as I don't paint anything on in layers. Perfectly peachy with me. Linzie Dockett wears so much makeup her face can't hold it all. It slides right off. By the end of the day she looks like a melted candle. Tucking my long, straight, dark hair behind my ears, I flip the visor up. I make a point to sit up tall so my mom won't go bonkers again. The Hummer's brake lights go off. Here we go!

I open the glove compartment and reach for the letter, birth certificates, and passports. We are moving forward. My mom hits the button to lower her window and turns to me for the documents. Out her open window, I see the redbrick wall come into view then the frame of a window, the front of a dark uniform, a window frame again, more red bricks . . .

We're still rolling. Oh no! We're rolling into Canada!

"Mooom!" I cry.

She slams on the brakes, pitching us all forward. I bang my elbow on the dash and my knee on the cup holder. My phone goes airborne.

"Oops," says my mom. "My bracelet got caught in the door handle. Everyone okay?"

"Yep," says Wyatt, laughing.

"Yes," I say, not laughing.

Sticking her head out the window, my mom yells back to the border patrol officer, "Sorry. Do you want me to back up into the US?"

I slap a hand over my eyes.

I. Am. Dying.

I hope they don't haul my mom off to border jail.

"Bit of a hurry?" The officer has come out of her little building. I can't see her face, but I hear her chuckling. The silver name tag on her pocket says CORRIGAN.

"Really, really sorry about that," my mom says meekly, handing her the passports.

"Where are you headed?" asks Officer Corrigan.

"Blackcomb Creek Lodge. Whistler. British Columbia."

She had to add the "BC"? My mom sounds stiff. Worried. Guilty.

"These are your children?"

"Yes, indeedy. Mine. All mine. Nobody else's."

We're doomed.

The officer bends to peer into the car. "Your full names and ages, please."

"Kestrel Lark Adams," I say coolly to show Mom how it's done. "I'm twelve."

"Wyatt Keith Adams," spouts my little brother. "I'm eight and one-quarter."

"Here are their birth certificates and parental permission letter from their father," says Mom. "My husband couldn't get away from work, but he'll be coming up soon."

I look away so the officer does not see me roll my eyes up into the far reaches of my head. Dad is *not* coming.

"And how long will you be in Canada?" asks the officer.

My head swivels. *Yes, mother, how long* will *we be in Canada?*

Giving me a sidelong glance, my mom leans toward the officer. I lean with her, so I can hear her whisper, "A month or two."

A squeak escapes my lips. A month? Or *two*?

"One moment." The officer steps back into the building with our documents.

"Mom!" I hiss. "Two months? That's the whole summer. You didn't say anything about staying all summer."

"I thought you might not want to come if you knew we might be here that long."

Ya think? The stabbing pain behind my eye is getting worse. My neck hurts now too. I think I have whiplash, thanks to my mom's little braking incident.

Officer Corrigan is back, handing the documents to my mom. An index finger points toward Canada. "*Now* you can be on your way."

As we chug up the hill past the Christmas-tree café, I

take a deep breath. We did it. We made it. We're in Canada.

"I'm hungry," announces Wyatt. "I hope they have normal food here." By "normal food," he means hamburgers, pizza, and junk.

"I'm sure they do," says my mom. "Unfortunately."

Before we reach the top of the hill, I take one last look back.

Good-bye, United States of America.

Good-bye, Langley and Annabeth.

Good-bye, only summer before seventh grade.

2
Don't Look Down!

Did you guys see that?" Wyatt's face hovers near my left shoulder. "That speed limit sign said one hundred. I love Canada! Floor it, Mom!"

"That's not miles per hour," I say, turning. "It's *kilometers* per hour. Canada's metric."

"Metric?" Wyatt crinkles his nose. "Well, how fast *is* one hundred kilometers per hour?"

Mom glances down at her speedometer, with its readout in both miles and kilometers. "Let's see, one hundred kilometers per hour is a little over sixty miles per hour."

With a grunt, my brother collapses into his seat.

We're driving west on Highway 1 toward Vancouver. The farms and pastures have given way to warehouses, gas stations, and strip malls, like back home. Every few miles there is an exit to the suburbs, like back home. Even the freeway signs are green with white lettering, like back home. So far, Canada doesn't look much different from the US. I don't know what I was expecting; munchkins and a yellow brick road, maybe?

"Kestrel, look!" Mom points up.

A green-and-white sign reads LANGLEY, NEXT EXIT.

"Langley!" I fumble for my phone to snap a photo, but it's too late. "Shoot," I say as the signs swishes past. My best friend would have loved that.

"We'll get one on the way home," says my mother.

I give the quickest of nods and slide down in my seat.

She cyes me. "Not talking to me, eh?"

"I'm talking," I say sincerely. I don't want to spend the whole trip being mad. I wish she had trusted me enough to be honest with me. Mom could have told me that we might be staying the whole summer in Canada. Okay, I might have been upset, but I wouldn't have thrown a tantrum or anything. I'm twelve, not two!

With a few more miles behind us, the freeway begins a long descent into a valley. We go beneath an overpass and there, directly in our path, a white harp rises five hundred feet into the sky! I try to blink it away because I am sure it can't possibly be a real musical instrument, but instead of disappearing, it multiplies. Now there are two giant white harps! *What is going on?* The freeway bends and both harps come into full view, one behind the other, and it all makes sense. The harps are a pair of tall cement towers shooting up from the middle of an arched bridge. Dozens of white steel cables fan out from the sides of each tower. The cables connect to the bridge deck below, creating two huge triangles. Beneath the bridge—far, far beneath—swirl the bluish-green waters of a wide river.

Wyatt whistles. "Cool."

"We're going on that?" I gulp, even as we start up the ramp. Heights make me jittery and dizzy and nauseous. I avoid Ferris wheels, ladders, rooftops, railings, the second floor of the mall, and pretty much anything that is taller than I am, which is pretty much everything.

We are closing in on the harps, cruising up and up and up. Why is my mother going so fast? My heart skips one beat. Then two. I clutch the door handle with both hands. I hope it's locked. We fly under the cables of the first tower and it is like entering the bones of an enormous teepee. I gaze up into a milky sky. Cable lines whip past. So fast. Too fast.

Bip, bip, bip, bip, bip, bip. The flicker makes my eyes hurt. I feel funny. Light-headed. Tingly.

"That's the Fraser River below us," says my mom.

I glance down. Big mistake. My head starts to spin. Counterclockwise, I think. It twirls faster and faster. I don't know where to look. I can't seem to focus on any one thing. The colorless sky, the choppy waters, the ripple of cables—everything is gyrating out of control. I can't breathe. My heart is hammering against my rib cage. *Let me out! Let me out!* I taste something sour. I may throw up. Or pass out. Or pee.

"You okay, Little Bird?"

"Nuh-uh." *Is that my voice? It sounds weak. Faraway.*

"Sit back. Close your eyes," says my mother. I don't know how she can be so calm considering we are about to plunge two hundred feet into the river. Oops. We're in Canada. It's meters. I don't know what that is in meters. It probably doesn't matter when you're *dead*, does it?

"Kestrel," her voice is firmer. "*Sit back.* Close your eyes."

I force my fingers to release the door handle. Leaning back, I clamp my eyes shut.

"Good girl," she says. "Inhale to the count of five. Now exhale. Five, four, three, two, one. Again. Slow breath in. Slow breath out."

I flutter my eyelids, but she says, "Keep them closed."

It takes a few minutes, but my heart rate slows. My stomach settles. Feeling gradually returns to my hands and feet.

Her hand is on my knee. "Better?"

"I think so." I open my eyes. We are no longer on the bridge.

"Keep breathing," she says. "Slow breath in. Slow breath

out. Good. Let your mind help you gain control over your body. You're doing fine."

Am I?

"Once we get to Vancouver, we'll head north on Highway Ninety-nine," she says. "It's called the Sea-to-Sky Highway, because it stretches from Howe Sound all the way up into the Coast Mountains to Whistler, Pemberton, and beyond. . . ."

I know she is talking to take my mind off things, so I close my eyes again and try to relax.

"It's a great drive. . . ." Her voice is soft against the hum of the engine. "Wait until you see it—the water, the islands, the mountains. Howe Sound is one of the most beautiful places on Earth. . . . You'll see. Sleep, Little Bird. . . . We'll be there soon. . . ."

My face feels warm. Sunlight flashes red and white against my eyelids. I open my eyes. My right shoulder is wedged between the seat and the window. My arm is bent awkwardly under me, one hand supporting my chin. Is that drool on my palm? Ew. I unfold myself. I don't know how long I've been asleep, but it must have been a while, because the world is different. The concrete barriers, warehouses, and strip malls are gone. We are on a four-lane highway, winding between rocky cliffs on my side and a sapphire sea on Mom's. The sky has cleared to a cerulean blue, and the navy-blue waters sparkle in the midday sun. Small, rocky islands break through the calm sea like a pod of surfacing whales. Deep green, tree-covered hills rise up from the opposite shore, jagged gray-and-white mountain peaks peering between them. This must be Howe Sound. My mother was right. It *is* beautiful.

I rub my neck. "Did we pass Vancouver?"

"About a half hour ago," Mom says quietly.

I turn in my seat. Wyatt is conked out.

"Mom?"

"Mmm-hmm?"

"Sorry about weirding out back there. Heights make me so—"

"It's all right. Port Mann *is* a tall bridge. I was a bit shaky up there myself."

I wasn't a bit shaky. I was petrified. And I hate that I was so scared.

My mother watches a sailboat slice through the glittering, white path of sun on the water, and her lips turn up. With each mile, the opposite shore gets closer, the hills higher. The sea narrows, turning from a deep blue to a milky turquoise. I comment on the beauty of the aqua color of the water, and my mom's smile fades. "It's the mineral deposits," she says. "They used to mine the rock in these hills, process it, and dump the waste into the water—copper, cadmium, iron, zinc."

"That sounds a little toxic."

"Try *a lot* toxic. The Sound was a marine dead zone for a long, long time. It's starting to rebound, though it's taken decades to clean up. With his Squamish heritage, your dad was hired to represent some of the aboriginal tribes some years back in a lawsuit against the government."

"And?"

"He won, though it took him a long time. Even now, it's a constant fight to keep the habitat pristine," she says.

"For every battle won, another company steps in to try to exploit the resources. The latest proposal will build a liquefied natural gas plant on one of the old timber mill sites. Grandma Lark sent me the link to the project opponents. They say it will dump hot, chlorinated water into the Sound."

"That's awful! Why would they do that?"

She sighs. "Greed. Money. Power. The usual reasons."

I stretch my neck to look out over the dash at the vast sea. It's as if ten thousand blue diamonds are sparkling. "Don't they know when we destroy habitats like this one, we are destroying ourselves?"

"You sound like your dad. You'd make a good environmental lawyer, Kestrel."

"Maybe," I say, but I'm not sure I want a job where I never get to see my family.

We follow the shore, the highway rolling left, then right, until Howe Sound ends in a U-shaped bay in the mining town of Squamish.

"There's the old Britannia Mine." Mom points to a big, ugly, gray, terraced building that looks to be growing out of the granite hillside. "It's a museum now."

We stop at a red light, our first full stop since before we crossed the border. My mother tips her head toward the opposite side of the street. She giggles. It's a McDonald's. I giggle too. Wyatt will be thrilled.

"Take a break or keep going?" she asks.

My butt's numb, and I have a cramp in my foot, but I am *so* ready for this trip to end.

"Keep going," I say.

We leave turquoise Howe Sound and the golden arches behind and begin climbing into the mountains. The road curves in *Ss* between slabs of sharp, golden rock. The trees get taller and slimmer as we go. Enormous, UFO-shaped clouds appear out of nowhere. They bunch up, casting long shadows over the slopes. As we go, more and more cabins dot the hills. The speed limit drops to fifty kilometers. Before I can ask my mom to translate the speed, I spot a tall, dark brown sign with white letters: WELCOME TO WHISTLER.

"We're here!" I cry.

"We're here?" Wyatt says in a groggy voice.

"We're here," sighs my mother.

We follow the directions on the GPS for a few more miles then turn into the main village. Traffic is, suddenly, heavy. It's like Christmas at the mall—except this mall is in the mountains. We crawl past condos, hotels, restaurants, and shops and sidewalks filled with people.

"There's the aboriginal center," says Mom, pointing to the modern, three-story glass building. "You'll be able to learn about your ancestry there."

Turning onto Blackcomb Way, we pass more hotels, condos, and a golf course. The road gets thinner as we wind our way toward the outer edges of the village. Mom makes a right onto Painted Cliff Road. We navigate about six or seven hairpin turns, then Wyatt's head appears at my shoulder. "There!" he calls, pointing.

To the left, I see a large, granite bolder with black metal script lettering: BLACKCOMB CREEK LODGE. Above the letters flies a bird, also black and metal. Mom turns onto a blacktopped driveway, and we weave through a forest of cedars, firs, pines, and hemlocks so tall and thick they nearly block out the sun. Soon, the cement ends and we are rolling across a patchwork of flat, sand-colored stones, sparkling with flecks of silver and gold. The trees part and we get our first glimpse of the lodge. My breath catches. When you think of a lodge, you think drafty cabins and broken cots and stinky outhouses . . . but this . . . this is amazing!

The lodge is old-fashioned and modern at the same time. It looks like a country church, but made from whole logs instead of flat, cut wood. Mammoth panels of glass create the A-framed front, rising fifty feet high. The tinted glass reflects the green boughs of the fir and pine branches that strain to touch them. Fanning out from the middle A-frame are two wings of rooms, each three stories high. The wings are supported by giant river-rock columns. Almost every room has a deck with dozens and dozens of red and white geraniums spilling over the wrought iron railings.

"Cool!" shouts Wyatt.

"It looks like something a Hollywood actor would live in," I say, snapping a few photos with my phone.

"Only this place is way bigger," says Wyatt.

My mom pulls to a stop under the covered entryway. The arched oak doors are intricately carved with aboriginal animals. From here, I can see the eagle wings, a deer's head, and bear paws. I open my door and get out. The air is cool, almost like it is at the ocean, except instead of salt, I inhale the scent of pine and sweet, damp earth. The only sound I hear is the wind rustling leaves and a few chirping songbirds. After three hours of riding in the car, my legs are wobbly. It takes me a minute to get used to gravity again. Not Wyatt. He is already dragging his Spider-Man suitcase out of the trunk.

"Hold on, son," says Mom, hurrying after him.

I push my arms above my head. My back cracks. I lean left. Then right. My teeth feel crusty. "Dibs on the shower." I shuffle to the back of the car.

A boy is rolling a luggage cart toward us. He's thin, but not skinny, and a head taller (okay, maybe two heads taller) than me. He looks a little older, too. He's wearing black pants and a white button-down shirt with the sleeves rolled up his forearms. I see a name tag pinned to his shirt, but I'm not close enough to read it. He flicks back a thatch of thick, chestnut hair and his dark eyes peer into mine. "Welcome to Blackcomb Creek Lodge."

"Thanks," I say.

"Cute," mutters my mother, elbowing me.

I hope he didn't hear her. I also hope I don't look as icky as I feel. Not that I am at all into boys. Okay, maybe a little. I did have a crush on Josh Luckinbill in history last year. I don't think he knew. I'm not ready for anything more than a secret crush. Still, you can't help thinking about them— boys, I mean. You know, for someday, when you *are* ready.

Mom turns to the bellboy. "We're Lark and Keith's family."

"She'll be happy to see you." He takes Wyatt's suitcase and places it onto the cart. "How was the drive up?"

"Long!" Mom and I say at the same time.

His grin deepens, and a little dimple appears on each side of his mouth. My knees feel wobbly. Still getting used to gravity, I guess.

"If you'd like to go on inside and get settled, I can handle things here," he says.

"Sounds good," says my mom. She reaches for her purse. "Oh, I don't have any Canadian money yet."

"American is fine," he says.

Mom hands him a few dollar bills. "Thank you . . . uh . . ."

"Breck," he says, tapping his name tag. He takes the tip. "Thank *you*."

Turning, she wiggles her eyebrows at me as if to say, *Cute name, too.* Oh, geez.

"Wyatt, let's go!" cries Mom, because my brother is already galloping through the trees like a knight on a horse. She heads toward the heavy, oak doors, then turns. "Little Bird, could you grab the passports and documents? I don't want to leave them in the car."

"Sure, Mom."

Reaching into the trunk for our picnic basket, Breck chuckles. "Little Bird?"

"It's a nickname." I can feel my neck getting warm. "My name is Kestrel."

"Nice to meet you."

"See, a kestrel is a— "

"A falcon, I know."

"You do? Sorry. Most people don't—"

"Do much hiking? Know about raptors? Live at the base of a twenty-four-hundred-meter mountain?"

"All of the above," I say.

He shuts the trunk. "Then this is your lucky day."

I can see his name tag now. BRECK McKINNON. It *is* a cute name. It dawns on me that my eyes don't hurt anymore. Not a bit. My headache is gone.

Breck starts pulling the luggage cart toward the lodge. "Don't forget the passports, Little Bird."

I can feel my cheeks getting lobster red. "I won't."

Now, if only I could remember where they are.

3

Dare to Keep My Power

K estrel!"

I catch a glimpse of a cobalt-blue shirt and black pants before I am pulled into a hug. After a long minute of Grandma Lark squeezing me and me squeezing her, we let go to get our first good look at each other. My grandmother is slim, yet athletic, and several inches taller than me, but then, who isn't? Her angel-white hair is short, yet styled in a fun, messy crop. Her eyes are a deep Spanish moss green, like mine, and her olive skin is smooth, also like mine. She smiles and there's only a faint hint of crow's-feet at the outer corners of her eyes. She's wearing a swish of coral lip gloss and hardly any blush or mascara. Not that she needs makeup. She is beautiful.

"You're stunning, Kestrel," she says, smoothing my shiny black hair over my shoulders.

"You too," I say.

"And so grown-up."

"You too," I blurt by mistake.

She lets out a laugh. "It's so good to have you all here. It's been a tough go these past few months."

"I can't even imagine, Lark," says Mom. "We're here to help in any way we can."

"That's right," I say. I may not have been thrilled about coming, but whining is one of my pet peeves. That and apathy. You need to care about things and then be willing to work to change them or nothing will ever get better. I learned that from my dad. He's a hard worker, and I admire him for that. I only wish he had time for us, too.

Wyatt runs his hand along one of the maple syrup–colored logs in the wall. "I feel like one of the Keebler elves."

Grandma, Mom, and I chuckle, but he has a point. The place is almost entirely wood. The high walls are constructed from rows and rows of enormous logs. Long, flat timbers crisscross the vaulted wood ceiling. The curving staircase in the center of the lobby has a log banister with log rails that circle up to the second and third floors—even the steps are built from smaller logs split in the middle. The fireplace is made of thousands of small, stacked, round river rocks, and the flagstone floor, with its big chunks of flat gold rocks, matches the driveway.

"Dad's gonna be sorry he missed this," says Wyatt, trotting off to explore the lobby.

"How *is* Cole?" Saying her son's name makes my grandmother's eyes brighten.

"Copacetic," says Mom. It means "okay," but when my mom uses it, it's code for *I don't want to talk about it, so please move on.* I think she figures using a fancy word will keep you from pressing things.

"Working on a big case?" asks Grandma Lark, unaware of my mother's verbiage traditions.

"He's up to his eyeballs in petroleum rights, but he sends his love," says my mom. "Once things quiet down, I'm sure he'll be up for a long weekend."

"Of course," says Grandma, but her eyebrows squiggle downward. *Hey, that's my* look.

While Mom and Grandma Lark chat, I take a few pictures. I point my phone straight up to get a shot of the round, black iron chandelier swinging from one of the beams. The metal ring holds a couple dozen fake candle lights. They are dripping fake wax. I text Langley: I made it! Here's the Lodge. What do you think? I attach the photos, including the exterior shots, and send the text.

Nicer than I expected, she replies in less than a minute. Any cute boys?

If I tell Langley about Breck, she'll want to know all kinds of details about him that I don't know and will probably never know, so there's no point starting that conversation. No, I lie. It is my last lie. I promise.

A young woman slides a plastic card across the desk. "Your key, miss," she says to me, her long, honey-brown ponytail swinging. She has pale skin and cherry-red lips. Mom would have a freak-fest if I wore that much lipstick. Her name tag reads DINAH STERLING. She slides a key card to Mom, too. "You're in the Alpine Suite on the third floor, Mrs. Adams—"

"A suite? Oh no, we couldn't," says my mother.

"Oh yes, you could," says Grandma Lark.

"Are you on the third floor too, Grandma?" I ask.

"No, hon. I have a small cottage out back, up the hill a few hundred meters." She checks her watch. "Listen, I've got a meeting, but let's have dinner together. I'll meet you in the dining room at, say, six o'clock? Our executive chef is preparing something special for your arrival."

"He shouldn't go to any trouble," says Mom.

"*She* should," says my grandmother. "How often does family come to visit?"

"Not often enough," says my mother apologetically.

"You're here now." The creases around Grandma's eyes deepen. "Talia McKinnon is our top chef and she's fantastic."

I glance up from my phone. "McKinnon? Is she related to Breck?"

"She's his mom," answers Grandma Lark. "We're all one big family around here. Now if you need anything, anything at all, please ask Dinah or Jess—Jess, where are you?"

An older, plump man in a blue cardigan, crisp white shirt, and a red bow tie appears in the office doorway. His curly hair is the color of an overly ripe peach. "Right here, oh fearless leader," he says with a grin. His name tag reads JESS GILBERTSON.

"Dinah and Jess are my right and left hands at the front desk," says my grandmother. "I don't know what I'd do without them."

The pair beams with pride.

Dinah gives us directions to our suite, and we say our good-byes.

"Wyatt, let's go!" calls Mom, heading for the elevator.

My little brother has his head in the big fireplace. It's okay. The thing is not lit.

In the elevator, I text Langley: We get a suite!

She replies: Sweet! Get it? I get it.

My mom unlocks the door. Our luggage is already inside the room, stacked neatly in the closet by the door. Our suite is spacious, yet cozy. The entry hall opens into a sitting room with two espresso-brown leather sofas and a well-shellacked tree-trunk coffee table. There's a big basket of fruit waiting for us. Off the sitting room are three bedrooms. I take the one that faces east, toward the summit, though I don't see much of the mountain from my window. My view is mostly fir trees. My room has fern-print curtains with a matching bedspread on a—what else?—log bed. I take a hot shower and put on a fresh pair of jeans with my favorite mint-green tee, which says HAPPINESS IS A CHOICE. In the sitting room, Wyatt is watching TV and eating a banana.

"Already broken into the fruit basket, I see," I tease.

"Mom said it was okay," he says, his mouth full.

Our mother's bedroom door is closed. She's probably taking a nap. I grab a red apple from the basket. "I'm going for a walk," I say to Wyatt. "Tell Mom I'll be back before we have to go meet Grandma."

He grunts.

Once I leave our suite, I can either head down the curved staircase to the second floor or go down the hall to the south wing. Part of the hall is a catwalk. It stretches across the open ceiling between the two wings and looks out over the lobby. It's a little high for me. Instead, I slip into a nook in the corner next to the elevator. I keep away from the railing. From here, I can see everything going on in the lobby below, but I'm not close to the edge. I'm in the shadows, so it's not easy for anyone glancing up to see me. This is how I am most comfortable: watching a world that can't watch back.

A young couple strolls in the main entrance. She is holding his arm as if he is the last life preserver on the *Titanic*. Newlyweds, I bet. They stop to talk to Jess. A side door near the fireplace opens. Breck appears, a garment bag over one arm. He goes beneath the stairs and I lose sight of him. One floor below me, a housekeeper rolls a cart across the catwalk. I slowly eat my apple. Is this what it's going to be like *all* summer? Yawn-o-rama. I check my phone for messages. Nothing from Annabeth or Langley. I wonder what they are doing right now. I bet it's a lot more exciting than what I'm doing. I take another bite of apple.

Ding!

Behind me, the elevator door slides open. It's too late to scurry back to the room or slip down the stairs, so I pretend to be oh-so-interested in my apple.

Breck steps off the elevator. He's still got the garment bag. "Fly on the wall, eh?"

I've been caught. I feel my face broil. He's going to think I have a skin condition. Maybe I do. Lobsteritis, caused by extreme embarrassment. Incurable.

"It's a great spot for people-watching," he says. "Do you like to read?"

"Uh-huh."

"There's a library on the first floor. I can show you, if you want."

"Thanks." *Why not? I'm not doing much else.*

"One sec." Breck holds up the garment bag. "Got to make a delivery first." He motions for me to come along. I toss my apple core in the recycle bin and start to follow him.

Uh-oh. He's going across the catwalk to the south wing.

Halfway across, he turns. "You coming?"

"Uhhhh . . ." I lift my chin to peek over the railing, and the lobby sways to the right. "I'll wait for you."

Folding the garment bag over the rail, he comes back. "Scared of heights, eh?"

"No. Not at all. Of course not. I'm perfectly fine." I sound as goofy and guilty as my mother did at the border. And he isn't buying it.

"You might as well face it," he says softly. "It won't go away until you do."

He's right, but I am not ready to admit it. I hardly know the guy.

"Take hold," says Breck. He put his hands out, palms down.

I give him a suspicious glare.

"I won't scare you." Breck leans in. "I promise. Come on."

I don't want to do it, but it's either that or race off in the other direction and look like an idiot. I take his fingertips in mine. I hold on loosely. Very loosely.

"Now look at my hands and tell me what you see."

I snicker. "You're kidding."

"I am not. Look at my hands and describe what you see," he says as if dealing with a squirrelly toddler.

"O-kay. I see . . . surprise! I see ten fingers and ten fingernails. They're clean and neat, which is good because most boys do not clean under their fingernails, and that is *so* gross. I swear, Wyatt's growing potatoes under his nails. Let's see . . . The middle nail on your right hand is cut a little crooked."

"Good. Look closer. Keep talking."

I bend slightly. "Um . . . you've got a small cut on your left pinkie. You should put a bandage on that, you know. It's kind of red already and you don't want it to get infected."

"Thanks. I'll do that. The bandage thing, I mean. Now do the left hand."

"Really? Breck, I don't see—"

"Trust me."

"Okay. I see . . . uh . . . two, no, three freckles on the top of your left hand. If I connected them it would make the letter *J*. The knuckle on your index finger is a little pinker than your other knuckles."

"Is that everything?"

I scan both hands one more time. "Uh-huh, that's pretty much it."

Breaking our hold, Breck throws his arms wide. "Then we're done here."

I straighten and look around. Whoa! I am on the other side of the catwalk! "How did you . . . ?"

"Not me. You. You're the one that did it." Breck hurries back to snatch the garment bag off the rail. "See, it's all about power. If you focus on your fear, you give it power. It's like you let it have all of your energy. You let fear have control over you. But if you put your mind somewhere else—on something far away from what you're afraid of—you keep the power. You stay in control."

"So while my brain was busy studying your hands, my feet naturally followed you and—"

He stretches out an arm. "Ta-da!"

I lightly applaud. "Impressive."

"It's a rock-climbing trick. You know, I've seen rock climbing help a lot of people get over their fear of heights. I could take you sometime if you want."

"Climbing?" My stomach knots as I remember the sheer cliffs we passed on the way up. "We'll see."

We are at the end of the south hall at the Summit Suite. I hear voices inside. I stand slightly behind Breck. He knocks twice on the door.

"That's the door," barks a girl.

"So get it." It's another girl with a similar voice—probably sisters.

"You're closer!"

"It's your turn!"

They're sisters, all right.

"Puh-lease. You don't want to pay the pizza guy."

"It's your turn."

Breck and I exchange uncomfortable looks.

"So you . . . uh . . . like working here?" I ask to drown out the arguing.

"Uh-huh. The people are great. George and Kyle—the

other bellhops—are good guys. They're in high school. Plus, it's decent money. I could only work part-time until school let out, but now I'm full-time through the summer." He turns toward the door and mutters, "If we make it that long."

Make it that long? I am about to ask him what he means, but the dead bolt clicks and the door opens. A girl with wide blue eyes and streaky blond collarbone-length hair scowls at us. She is wearing a neon pink skirt and several layered tank tops—one light pink, one white, and one dark pink. The second she sees Breck, her big eyes get even bigger and that sour look of hers turns into the biggest, fakest smile I've ever seen. "Hiiiiii, Breck," she says.

"Hello, Miss Tolliver," Breck says evenly.

She flashes him a big smile. "I told you to call me Veranda."

"Check for olives," yells her sister. "I ordered olives last time and they forgot."

Veranda leans back. "It's not the pizza guy!"

Breck holds out the garment bag. "Dry cleaning for your mom."

Veranda takes the bag and tosses it over her shoulder. We watch it crumple into a pile on the floor.

"Hold on." Veranda leans out of sight then returns to hand Breck a folded Canadian dollar bill. It's a bright shamrock green, much prettier than the faded green of American money.

"Thank you," he says, backing up to leave.

"Wanna come in?" asks Veranda. "We ordered pizza, as you probably figured out thanks to big mouth back there, and it should be here soon."

"Sorry. Can't. Working."

"Quit flirting with the pizza guy, will you?" shouts Veranda's sister. "The pizza's getting cold."

"It's *not* the pizza, Rose!" screams Veranda, shattering our eardrums. She squints to read my HAPPINESS IS A CHOICE shirt then looks at me like I sneezed on her salad. "Seriously?"

"Seriously," I say. "I think no matter what situation you're in you can either make the best of it or the worst of it. It's up to you."

Ha! How's that for being truthful?

She pretends to yawn. "How annoyingly optimistic."

"It's more than that," I say. "'Life is what our thoughts make it.' I didn't say that. It's a quote from Marcus Aurelius the emperor. It's like when you take a test or have to talk in front of the class—"

"Or cross a high bridge," adds Breck.

"Or cross a high bridge," I say, feeling my lobsteritis flare up again. "Don't you usually *do* better when you *think* you can?"

"I guess," she says dismissively.

"Don't guess," I say. "*Know.* Guessing won't get you far in life."

"Excuse me?" The sour face is back. "Are you lecturing me?"

"Um . . . no. I'm sorry. I only meant—"

"Who lectures people they don't even know? How rude. Who *are* you, anyway?"

"I'm . . . I'm . . . I'm . . ."

I'm stuck is what I am.

"I could report you to the owner, you know. I could get you fired like that." Veranda snaps her fingers and I believe her. She searches my shirt for a name tag. "What's your name?"

"I'm starving here. . . ." A head pops out from behind the door. "Oh hiiiiii, Breck."

I jump back. Veranda and Rose aren't only sisters. They're twins!

"Hi, Rose," says Breck. He spins me around and points me toward the way we came. "Must be going. Have a nice day, ladies."

Veranda slams the door. Hard. The violent bang, and its vibration, rattle me to the core. Breck is pulling me so fast across the catwalk, I don't have time to be scared. "Are you always so blunt?" he asks.

"No," I say. "Apathy is one of my pet peeves."

"I'll remember that."

"I *am* sorry. Will you get in trouble?"

"Nah." He slows down once we are across the bridge. "Veranda and Rose are usually stomping their feet about something."

"I didn't mean to offend her."

"The Tollivers are one of the richest families in the province, which is probably why you got under Veranda's skin. In her world, happiness comes from a shopping bag. I can't say I agree with her, but . . ." He pulls his hand out of his pocket and unfolds the bright green dollar bill. I see a picture Queen Elizabeth and the numeral 20 in the lower right corner. ". . . she does tip well."

"Twenty dollars? For delivering dry cleaning?"

"Not bad, eh? I'll take you to the library now." His lips slip sideways. "It's a no-talking zone, so you should be able to stay out of trouble there." Breck reaches to punch the button for the elevator.

"Wait, Breck. I want to know what you meant when you said you'd be full-time through the summer, *if we make it that long.*"

"Uh . . . you heard that, huh?"

"Is something wrong? Does it have to do with my grandmother?"

"No," he says, but his head bobs. It's a total giveaway.

"Something *is* wrong. What is it?"

Breck shoves his hands in his pockets. He looks down. He shuffles his feet on the shiny oak floor. He is debating whether to tell me, and the longer he waits the more frightened I get. It must be bad.

"Please, tell me," I say. "It could take me all summer to figure it out, and by then it could be too late."

Breck lifts his head. Worried brown eyes gaze into mine. "Kestrel, it might already be too late."

4

Don't Get Involved in Adults' Problems

W hat do you mean *it might already be too late?*"

Breck holds up his finger to signal to wait until we are in the elevator. Once the door closes, he starts to explain. "Last fall, guests who'd booked for the ski season started calling to cancel. At first, it didn't seem like any big deal. You always get cancellations with flu and bad weather and all, but the cancellations kept coming and coming."

"Why?"

"That's the crazy part. Guests told Dinah and Jess that

they'd been called and told all kinds of things—that the roof had collapsed or we'd had a bedbug infestation, even that our dining room had been closed by the health department. That one wasn't true because I'd know about it, for sure. My mom is the executive chef here. They were all lies."

"Who was doing the calling?"

"Nobody knew. We never did find out. The worst part was . . ."

The elevator door slides open. An elderly man is standing there, waiting to get on. Breck gestures for me to go ahead of him. "The library is this way."

We hurry through the lobby, past the fireplace, bearing right. At the end of a short hallway, Breck turns left and we are, suddenly, surrounded by books. While Breck checks the stacks to make sure we are alone, I get my first good look around. The library is a little larger than your average classroom, with enough space for three rows of four-tiered, freestanding shelves. Next to the window, a pair of red-and-green plaid chairs face one another, an antique floor lamp with a stained-glass shade between them. Cute little green frogs are playing leapfrog around the rim of the shade.

Breck is back. "Anyway, so even though Jess, Dinah, and your grandmother did their best to try to clear things up, nobody believed them. I mean, if a hotel *does* have a bedbug infestation, it's not something they are going to admit, right? Most of the guests ended up canceling their reservations and booking somewhere else."

"Oh, no!"

"We all agreed somebody must have hacked into the computer system to get the guest list," says Breck. "Jess beefed up our online and in-house security, and we thought that was the end of it."

"It wasn't?"

"Nope." Breck took out his phone. "Over the past few months, someone's been posting fake negative reviews about the lodge on all the major travel sites on the Web. Check it out." He hands the phone to me. "Here's just one site."

"A one-star review? For this lodge? Are they nuts?"

"Scroll down."

They were *all* one-star reviews, and there must have been at least thirty of them.

"Read the comments," says Breck.

"'The rude bellhop put our luggage in the wrong taxi and we never saw it again.'" I slide to the next review. "'We could have played Twister with all the stains on the carpet. There were mice living in the closet!'" I let out a shriek. "Mice?"

"Shhh-shhh-shhh!" says Breck. "Lies, all lies. And for the record, George, Kyle, and I are not rude, and we have never lost a guest's suitcase."

"Look at this," I say, pointing to a picture of a run-down cabin with the caption, *Blackcomb Creek Lodge*. "It's not even this lodge."

"Welcome to our world."

"This is terrible."

"*This* could put us out of business."

I am in shock. Could Grandma actually lose this place?

"I've gotta get back to work," says Breck. "I don't know if I should have told you all this or not—"

"I'm glad you did. Thanks."

He gives me an uncertain nod, before leaving.

I am not sure what to do. Should I tell my mom? Should I say something to Grandma Lark? Maybe she doesn't want us to know. Is it even any of our business?

I am still wondering of what to do when we meet my grandmother for dinner. The dining room of the lodge is a lot like her: elegant but relaxed. The fifteen or so rectangular tables are made from sturdy, weathered cedar. Each is circled by a cluster of high-backed chairs upholstered in a nubby cream linen. The fabric matches the napkins we find folded into delicate swans on our pale blue plates. In the center of each table is a small blue glass vase that holds white wildflowers. Glass lights that remind me of half-moons drip from the ceiling, suspended by swirling bronze arms. They cast a dusty, golden glow over the room.

The newlyweds sit at a small table in the middle of the room near the see-through fireplace. A couple of older kids that look like they are in college are camped in the corner, their laptops open in front of them. Then there's the four of us—Wyatt and Mom on one side of the table, and Grandma

Lark and me on the other. We are near a wall of windows that looks west, out over a view of steep hills blanketed with fir trees and a deep blue lake shaped like a bunny's profile. The sun still hangs well above the slopes, but is beginning to paint streaks of rose and tangerine onto the long, flat clouds scattered across the sky.

Although the halibut and rosemary mashed potatoes are delicious, I spend most of dinner pushing them around my plate. I can't stop thinking about what Breck told me. It feels strange to be sitting here, pretending everything is all right, when my grandmother could be weeks away from closing the lodge. Isn't she going to tell us what's going on? And how long should I wait before I tell anybody what I know?

"Kestrel, answer your grandmother, please." Mom is staring at me.

"I'm . . . I'm sorry, what?"

"I was wondering if you didn't care for your food," says Grandma Lark. "You've hardly touched it. Talia can make something else for you, if you like."

I look down at my grilled halibut with apricot sauce and

flattened mashed potatoes. "No, I'm fine. The fish is good." It's true. "Guess I'm tired."

"I always have a hard time eating when I'm worn-out too," she says.

"Look at that sunset," says Mom with a sigh.

The sinking sun is kissing the tip of an arrowhead-shaped, snowcapped peak. It transforms the sky into an ombré canvas of deep orange, then magenta and lavender, and finally, sapphire. Wyatt is too busy playing a game on Mom's phone to look up.

"Grandpa Keith and I used to take the lift up Blackcomb to watch the sunset nearly every night in the summer," says Grandma Lark. "The wind would be whipping and I'd be all bundled up in my thick sweater and there would be my husband in his Hawaiian shirt, Bermuda shorts, and sandals, like we were on a beach in the Caribbean."

Mom and I grin.

"I'd be ready to come down, but he'd say, 'Let's wait another few minutes. We might see a green flash,' so, naturally, I'd stay."

"Green flash?" Wyatt's head pops up. "What's that?"

Grandma Lark leans forward as if about to reveal a secret. "As the sun sets, the very top edge will give off a bright green glow. It happens for only a second, and all the conditions have to be absolutely perfect for you to see it. The sky has to be clear—no clouds or pollution. Also, you have to be eye level with the horizon. A green flash is a rare phenomenon. You can spend your whole life watching sunsets and never see one."

"Have *you* ever seen one?" asks Wyatt.

"No. Your Grandpa Keith used to tease me plenty about it, though. We'd be up on Blackcomb enjoying the sunset, and all of a sudden, he'd say, 'There, Lark! A green flash! Did you see it?' Of course, I hadn't, and I doubt he had either, that rascal."

We chuckle.

"Still," she says, her gaze wandering out the window, "I like to think *maybe* he did see one before he left this Earth."

I watch as her moss-green eyes mist over.

"Awww," says my mother. She taps her heart but looks around uncomfortably.

Wyatt goes back to his game.

I want to say something to my grandmother to make her feel better, but I have no idea what. I've never had anybody I love die before. I've never even been around anybody who's ever had a loved one die before. What if I say the wrong thing? What if I make it worse? She has lost her husband, and she is about to lose her business. The last thing I want to do is make her life any worse. If only I knew her better.

"I could use more coffee," says Mom. "Lark?"

My grandmother says, "Sure," and Mom waves to Madeline, the waitress.

Grandma Lark's tan hand is resting on the creamy linen arm of her chair next to me. She is still wearing her wedding ring—a polished silver band inlaid with triangles of lapis and turquoise. The dark blues and bright aquas, divided by silver geometric lines, remind me of these mountains. The ring fits in a little divot of her skin as if it has always been there.

Slowly, 'cause I don't want to scare her, I reach to cover my grandmother's hand with my own. Her fingers are cool and still. In the rosy glow of the dining room, with newly-weds cuddling and people jabbering and the waitress refilling coffee cups, Grandma Lark's eyes meet mine. They sparkle with gratitude. A feeling of relief spreads through me. I haven't made things worse. Her lips are curling gently upward. So are mine.

"Mom, come see this!"

She leans out the doorway of the bathroom, a piece of floss dangling from her mouth. "What?"

I am sitting on the floor between the sofa and the tree-trunk coffee table, with my laptop open. "I'm on one of the travel sites Breck showed me." I start reading some of the comments to her. "'The housekeeping staff wouldn't give us fresh towels. My room smelled like stinky cheese.' Oh, this is a good one. 'I got sick on what passed for chili in their crummy dining room.'"

Snapping off the bathroom light, she scurries over. "What in the world . . . ?"

"They're all bad—at least, the ones posted within the

last six months. Before that, they're all four- and five-star reviews."

Mom sits on the sofa and starts to read over my shoulder. With each review, her mouth drops farther. "How can people get away with this?"

I shrug. "It's the Internet."

"That's no excuse. Look, this one says his room faced a brick wall. Not one single room here faces a wall. And who the heck is SkiBum1432, anyway? It's not fair. They don't even have to give their real names."

"Wait till you get to PoodleGirl29—"

"Arrrgggggh!"

She's there. "'Avoid Blackcomb Creek Lodge like the plague, unless you're into diseases, in which case you'll have plenty to choose from.' Ohh!" She jumps to her feet and starts pacing the room. "This is deliberate sabotage. I'd better get ahold of Lark's webmaster to get those awful reviews taken down."

"There's usually nothing you can do unless the reviews contain personal attacks," I say. "But something similar happened to Annabeth's dad's café, and he got his loyal customers to post a bunch of positive reviews and say the other reviews were lies—"

"While we're at it," she says, picking up speed, "it might be a good idea to give the whole site a fresh look—you know, with new photos and text. I wonder how long it's been since Lark updated it. I wonder if she even has a social media presence. It might be time to hire a marketing expert."

"Langley's mom works for a public relations company," I say. "I bet she could—"

"I'd better touch base with the tourism bureau here to see what we can do to jump-start business." Mom takes another lap. "It's too late for the summer season, but they might able to give us a hand booking conventions and retreats for next winter . . ."

I hold up my hand as she circles past. "Mom, what if we—"

"Honey, please, I can't think."

I let my hand drop.

My mom opens her laptop on the desk. "The first thing

I need to do is sit down with Lark and find out where things stand with the business."

"What can I do?" I ask.

"You've done plenty by bringing all of this to my attention. Thanks, hon. Why don't you go on to bed? It's getting late."

"O-kay." I turn off my computer.

I wish my mother would let me help. She still thinks of me as a little kid, even though I'll be thirteen in four months. I guess it's hard for her to see me as anything other than someone who needs looking after, like Wyatt, because that's what I have always been. My mom doesn't think I am grown-up enough to handle adult problems. I'm not saying she's wrong, but I'm not so sure she's right. Either way, wouldn't it be something to be treated as if I *were* old enough to understand, as if I *could* help? Because one day I will be, and maybe that day will come sooner than she thinks.

I tuck my laptop under my arm. "Good night, Mom."

"Night, Little Bird." Her fingers flying over the keyboard, she does not look up.

5

Dare to Admit It When Your Brother Is Right (Argh!)

"I still don't see why you're so down," says Langley, sweeping back her thick ginger hair. She bends toward her computer screen. "I would be thrilled if I got to spend the whole summer at a fantabulous ski lodge in the mountains with no responsibilities. Instead, I am stuck here cleaning out the refrigerator and picking slugs out of the garden, which, if you ask me, should be considered child abuse. And all because of you."

"Me? Why me?"

"Because the minute you left, my mom gave me a summer to-do list that is longer than my hair. Look at this. Just look at it!" She holds a piece of paper up to the screen. It's too close for me to read it, but I pretend I can.

"Sorry," I say. "I still think being bored is worse than being busy. We've been in Whistler a week, and the only thing my mom will let me do is babysit Wyatt. Yippee."

"If I get all my stuff done, Mom says I can go to the lake this afternoon."

"The lake?" My stomach pitches. Langley is going to Lake Wilderness. Without me. "Is Annabeth going too?" I ask, although I know the answer.

"Yes, but it won't be the same without you."

"Thanks."

"And I mean that in more ways than one. You know how Annabeth rows. We'll be going in circles all day."

We giggle.

"Oh, I forgot to tell you I saw Aaron Hasenbuhler at the store," she says.

Langley has been crushing on Aaron since March. It was a secret crush. All of our crushes are secret. We aren't brave enough to confess them to anyone but each other.

"Did you talk to him?" I ask, knowing full well she didn't. Neither of us has that much courage.

"Yes," she says.

"Nooooooo!" I almost topple off my bed, taking my laptop with me.

"I said I was going to the lake today and he said he might see me there because he wanted to go fishing and I said I liked fish and then I started blubbering something about 'but not tuna but that doesn't matter because there are no tuna in Lake Wilderness' and it got ugly from there. That boy is like cotton candy for the brain."

"The important thing is you did it. You were brave enough to talk to him."

"I did, didn't I?" She clasps her hands. "Aaron looks exactly like Caden Christopher, don't you think?"

"C . . . Caden Christopher?"

Is she serious? Aaron Hasenbuhler looks *nothing* like the most popular teenage singer in America. Caden is tall and has wavy blond hair. Aaron is short and has a brown crew cut. Caden has a dimpled jaw. Aaron has a pimpled jaw. Caden has ice-blue eyes. It's a little hard to tell what color Aaron's eyes are. His eyes are sort of hidden beneath two bushy eyebrows that are few hairs short of meeting in the middle. Still, Aaron is a nice guy, and Langley likes him, so why not?

"Uh . . . sure," I say. "They're practically twins." I shiver as Rose and Veranda's smug faces pop into my head.

"Did you hear his new release?" Langley is asking.

"Aaron's?" I tease.

"No!"

Of course I've heard it. He's my favorite singer too. "'Hangin' by a Thread' is crazy good," I say.

"'Still hanging by a thread from your heart.'" Langley sings the first line.

I chime in with the second line, "'You kept me on a string from the start.'"

We've always liked singing together. We've sung a duet in every school talent show since the fifth grade. For a moment, singing with her like this, it doesn't feel like we are 215 miles—I mean, 345 kilometers—apart.

"He wrote that song. He writes all his own songs," says Langley, and I believe her, because she knows everything there is to know about him. Sure, I like Caden Christopher, but I'm not obsessed—not the way Langley is. She knows weird facts about him, like his shoe size (10) and what he eats for breakfast (scrambled eggs). "He's coming this summer, you know," says Langley.

I choke. "To Seattle? Caden Christopher is coming to Seattle?"

"Yep. He's doing a whole West Coast tour of the US and Canada. My dad is going to try to get tickets for Annabeth and me. Want him to get one for you, too?"

I want to shout, *Yes, get me a ticket too!* but what if we're still stuck here? "Better not," I say. "I don't know when we'll be home."

"Let me know if things change. I'd better go. I want to get a run in this morning before I have to vacuum the *entire* house." She gags. "Have you been running?"

We are both on the cross-country team at school. We

are supposed to be running over the summer to stay in shape.

"I've done a couple of short runs on the street, but that's it." I roll my eyes. "Mom says I can't go on the trails by myself." I do miss it. I love to run. It clears my head and helps me think. Running makes me feel strong. Alive. Worthy.

"Maybe you can find someone to run with you, like a cute boy or something."

"Right," I say sarcastically, while trying to erase Breck's face from my mind. "Have fun at the lake," I say. "Call me if you need rescuing."

With a wave that makes her fingers go blurry, my best friend is gone.

"So, what's it going to be?" I ask Wyatt.

I am babysitting my brother. Again. Mom and Grandma Lark are meeting with the webmaster or somebody, but nobody is telling me anything about what is happening with the lodge. I am too young to be trusted. It's frustrating.

"I don't know." Wyatt groans, his body oozing over the arm of the chair.

"I promised Mom no TV or video games." I fan out the brochures on the tree-trunk coffee table. "It's your last day before you start Day Camp at Lost Lake tomorrow, so it's up to you. Choose one. It'll be fun."

Wyatt lets out a *poor me* sigh. To him, any day without TV or video games is *not* fun. He stares blankly at the flyers.

"Dinah says there's an arts-and-crafts fair in the village," I say.

"Nah."

"How about putt-putt golf?"

"Nah."

"What about this one?" I tap the flyer from the Squamish Lil'wat Cultural Centre. "I bet they have some great aboriginal masks and canoes, maybe even some weapons."

"Maybe," he says, barely glancing at the pamphlet.

"Come on, Wyatt, pick something."

"Let me see that one on the end."

Wouldn't you know he'd lock onto the one I was trying

to hide? He is gazing right, but I slide out the flyer on the left. "The Whistler Museum. Good choice—"

"Not that one, Kes. The one on the other side. Is that a bear?"

I pull out the green flyer from Kodiak Clem's Bear Tours. As soon as he sees the headline, his bones magically return. Wyatt grabs the pamphlet and starts to read. "'More than fifty black bears freely roam the Whistler-Blackcomb area.' Wow! *Fifty* bears. Did you know there were that many?"

I shake my head. Vigorously.

He keeps reading. "'Let one of our experienced guides show you the best viewing places for discovering these giants of the forest. From the comfort of a stylish Land Rover, your two-hour excur . . . excur . . .'"

"Excursion. It means trip."

"'Your two-hour excursion includes snacks, water, and some of the most scenic views around.' Let's do this, Kes. Let's go see some bears."

"I don't know, Wyatt. Look, it says on the back there's no guarantee you'll see any bears. We could drive all over the place for nothing. Besides, I bet they're probably already booked up today."

"Call. Find out. This is what I want to do."

I call. I find out. They aren't booked up. We are on the noon tour. Great.

Since we have some time to kill, we decide to take the trail down to the village. It's a sunny day, except for a few cottony clouds scooting across the sky. About halfway down the hill, we leave the sidewalk and follow the footpath short-cut through the woods. A few hundred yards later, we reach a marked fork in the trail. The top arrow on the sign reads LOST LAKE and points to the right, while the arrow below it points left and says WHISTLER VILLAGE. We turn left and go about a quarter mile before the trail ends on the sidewalk of Blackcomb Way near the aboriginal center. Wyatt and I cross the street, then go over the wooden footbridge above Fitzsimmons Creek. I keep to the center of the bridge. I count the lines on my knuckle as I walk, the way Breck taught me. It works. It's enough to distract me so I don't think about the bridge collapsing into the rushing river below. The path leads to some steps, which take us between a couple of hotels and into the main village. I love strolling the redbrick pedestrian-only streets, past the outdoor cafés and gift shops. Hotels and condos take up the second and third stories of the buildings, with the bigger hotels rising up around the village.

"Let's get a cone at Cows," says Wyatt.

We've only been in town for a week, but the ice cream store with the big black-and-white fiberglass cow statue out front is already our favorite place to go. Wyatt gets a waffle cone with birthday cake ice cream. It has confetti sprinkles and even smells like cake. Back home, I usually get strawberry cheesecake, but this time I try the Gooey Mooey: vanilla ice cream with toffee, chocolate chunks, and with a thick, swirling ribbon of caramel. It's delish—superrich, creamy, and true to its name, very gooey!

We eat our ice cream and slowly walk the Village Stroll—well, I eat and Wyatt inhales! He's done before we even make it a few blocks to the giant metal rings from the 2010 Winter Olympics. I snap a photo of my brother leaning on an outer ring before we circle back around the outer edge of the village.

While Wyatt drools over a BMX bike in the window of a bicycle shop, I finish my cone. I go to toss my napkin and paper into a recycle bin, but have to spend a minute figuring out how to put my hand into the handle to pop up the heavy, metal lid. A label on the hunter-green bin says it's bear-proof. Yikes. Do bears really come into the village?

I check my phone. It's twelve minutes after eleven. "Wyatt, we'd better go. We still have to get lunch before the bear tour—"

"Kes!" Wyatt is pointing across the square. "There's the gondola Grandma told us about that goes to the top of Whistler Mountain. We could go this afternoon when we get back from the bears. Wanna?"

"You want to go on . . . that?" Clinging by metal claws to a thin wire, the gondola cars glide up and down the mountainside. They look like giant ice cubes suspended one hundred feet off the ground.

"I can't wait to go," says Wyatt.

"I can," I say under my breath.

"Grandma says there's another gondola at the top that

takes you from Whistler over to Blackcomb Peak."

"Seriously? *Across* the valley?"

"It's called the Peak 2 Peak. How cool is that? Some of the cars have glass floors!"

"Do not."

"Do so. Grandma said."

Glass floors? My heart starts to pound.

"Sorry, Wyatt," I say. "I can't take you. Not now. Not ever." I twirl and zoom across the square as fast as two trembling legs can carry me.

Wyatt catches up. "Why not?"

"You know why."

He sighs. "Aren't you over that yet?"

I don't answer.

"It's no big deal. Mom's scared of bees," he says. "Dad hates driving next to big trucks. I flip out if I have to get a shot at the doctor's—"

"I get it, Wyatt. Everybody has fears. Thanks," I clip.

"So you'd be afraid to be that high off the ground. Then what?"

I glare at him. "Isn't that enough?"

He lowers his head and starts kicking a pebble over the red brick walkway. Thank goodness that conversation is over. We head back across the wooden bridge above Fitzsimmons Creek. This time, I move a little closer to the railing—not much, but a little.

My brother is tugging on my shirt. "Hey, Kes, remember last year, at Elvin's birthday party, when we went to Northwest Trek and everybody was going on the zip line? I was super scared, and I didn't want to go."

"I remember."

"I got all dizzy—"

"And you got a bellyache," I recall.

"And my knees got all noodly."

"You were sure you were gonna die." I think I am proving my point here.

"But I didn't." Wyatt stops on the trail. "I felt horrible, like I was *gonna* die, but nothing bad happened. In fact, I ended up going on the zip line *three* times that day. Don't you get it, Kes?"

I do. Sort of. "So you're saying fear can't kill you, it just makes you *think* it can?"

"Bingo."

I never thought about it like that before. When you hate all the things being afraid makes you feel—the pounding heart, the shortness of breath, the spinning head—it's only natural to do whatever you can to escape it. But what if you didn't try to outrun it? What if you stood fast, faced your fear, and said, "Okay, bring it on"? What then? I don't know, but it might be worth a try. I look at my little brother, with his messy hair, scraped elbows, and streak of birthday cake ice cream on his chin. "You know something, Wyatt Keith Adams? You're a pretty smart kid."

He folds his arms in front of him and, for the first time in his eight and one-quarter years, does not grunt.

6

Don't Go on a Bear Tour with Evil Twins (but If You Must, Do Not Sit between Them)

"I'd like a hot dog and fries, please," Wyatt says to Madeline. "No ketchup. Extra mustard."

"I'll have a B.L.T.A.," I say. That's a bacon, lettuce, tomato, and avocado croissant sandwich. We each order an orange soda.

There is only one person in the dining room with us: a man—in his forties, I'd guess. He's eating a heaping salad covered in so much ranch dressing it looks like a mountain in winter. He's spilled some dressing on the front of his olive safari shirt. The shirt has pockets everywhere, even on the shoulders. His shorts match his shirt: olive, with zillions of pockets. We finish lunch, and I pay the bill with money Mom gave me. Wyatt and I go to the lobby to wait for the bear tour people to pick us up. We're a few minutes early. I am so nervous I have to go to the restroom to pee four times.

"Is this bear tour thing okay for Wyatt?" I ask Dinah on my last trip back from the restroom. "He's just a kid."

"Oh, yes," she says. "He'll love it. You get to go off-road and everything."

"Off-road? How far off-road?"

She tips her head toward the door. "You'll see."

A gigantic, lime-green Land Rover with a photo of a black bear running across one side of the vehicle is pulling up. KODIAK CLEM'S BEAR TOURS is plastered over the doors in bright yellow letters.

"I get the front!" cries Wyatt, tearing for the car.

"If we don't make it back, tell my mom and grandma I love them," I say to Dinah.

The corners of her cherry-red lips turn up. "You'll be fine."

I get in the car behind the driver so I can keep an eye on my brother. There are already three other people in the vehicle: a married couple in the very back and a man in his late twenties behind me. He's got a camera and a lens so large it needs its own seat!

"Hey there, missy." The muscular driver is glancing at me in the rearview mirror. Sunglasses shaped like alien eyes and a straggly beard cover most of his face. He's wearing a dark brown leather cowboy hat with red braid around the trim and a khaki shirt with the sleeves pushed up to his bulging biceps. The driver looks at a sheet of paper taped to the dash. "You must be Lark's grandkids."

My brother thumps his chest. "I'm Wyatt. She's Kestrel. Are you Clem?"

"Nope. I'm Mutt. Clem's driving our other vehicle. We'll meet up at Widowmaker Ridge. It's a rule that we always travel together in case something happens."

Widowmaker Ridge? In case something happens? I have to pee again.

Wyatt is firing questions at Mutt. "Have you ever been

chased by a bear? How far up the mountain do we go? How many bears do you think we'll see?"

Mutt keeps up. "Chased? Nah. I have enough sense to keep my distance, unlike some of the tourists, who treat bears like puppies. Big mistake. Always respect wildlife, son. We're going up about six hundred meters or so. No telling how many bears we'll come across, but this morning we saw a big fella catching fish at Slippery Creek."

"Wicked!" Wyatt does a rooster neck bob. "I hope we see lots of bears."

I hope we don't. I so hope we don't.

My window is down. Closing my eyes, I take a big gulp of crisp mountain air. I hear the lodge door creak open.

"Hold my lip gloss? I don't have pockets."

"Neither do I."

"Then what is that thing sewn on the side of your sweater?"

"A decorative accent."

"Come on—"

"No! I don't want your makeup stretching out my clothes."

I'd recognize that bickering anywhere. I open my eyes. Rose and Veranda are marching toward us. Veranda is wearing a pink cardigan with the sleeves pushed up, a pink lace tee, jeans, and a ball cap covered in pink rhinestones. Her pink beaded sandals go *spick-spack* against the flagstone. Rose has on a white boatneck top with thin, navy horizontal stripes, white shorts, and white tennis shoes without socks. *Please let them be going shopping or out to lunch or anywhere that isn't—*

My car door opens.

With us. They are coming with us. I knew this was a bad idea.

"Hi." Rose smacks her gum. "Could you scoot over?"

I start to slide across the seat. Before I can make it to the other side, Veranda flings open that door and hops in. I am trapped between the Tolliver twins.

"Oh goody, it's Happiness Girl," Veranda murmurs. "Here to spread more joy?"

I pretend not to hear that.

"Guess not," she spits, fixing her hair. A wide gold bracelet with three rows of diamonds slides down her arm. "Oops. I shouldn't guess. I should *know*."

I have a feeling this is going to be the longest ride of my life.

"Hello, ladies," says Mutt. "Either you're the Tollivers or I'm seeing double."

Everyone laughs. I try to laugh too, but can't. I know too much.

"Fasten your seat belts, folks." Mutt's voice booms through the SUV.

I click in my seat belt, and we are off. We turn left out of the driveway and head up Painted Cliff Road. This is it. We are going up the mountain to search for bears. I'd give anything to be at Lake Wilderness with Langley and Annabeth right now. Veranda and Rose are taking out their phones. Their red cases glimmer with what I can only assume are genuine rubies. I slip out my own phone. It's in a yellow plastic case with an owl on the back. Veranda sneaks a look at my phone. She squishes in her lips as if I'm holding a tarantula.

I text Langley: I am on a bear tour with Wyatt. That's right, we are going LOOKING for bears! Can you believe that?

I stare at my phone for several minutes, but she doesn't text back.

Rose tips her head to look at me. "You're American, aren't you?" When I nod, she says, "I could tell by your accent."

I have an accent? I guess I shouldn't be surprised. I've noticed slight differences in the way Canadians speak too. My grandmother and Dinah pinch off their words, like they are forming them at the back of the throat instead of on the tongue. It gives them kind of a nasal sound. They pronounce words differently too. When I say the word "been," it sounds like "ben." When they say it, it's "bean." "Out" is "owt" for me and "oot" for them.

We are winding our way up the mountain. After about a kilometer or so, the smooth pavement abruptly ends. The Land Rover bounces onto a dirt road, although I'm not sure the word "road" is even remotely accurate. It's more like an overgrown dirt path with the biggest bumps and deepest ruts known to humanity. Now I know what Dinah meant when she said "off-road." One second we are being thrown from side to side, and the next we are thumping our heads on the ceiling. If there are *any* bears out here, we're all bucking around too much to spot them. My stomach is tumbling like a clothes dryer, and I keep banging my right knee on my brother's seat. Wyatt, however, is having the time of his life. He's got his hands spread out on the dashboard for stability, his head tracking right and left as he scopes the forest for bears.

"Bear Two calling Bear One," Mutt says into his radio. "Do you read? Over."

The radio crackles. "Bear Two, this is Bear One. We're on the north side of Widowmaker Ridge at the hairpin turn above Vista Lake. We've got a mama bear and two cubs within sight. Over."

"We're on our way," says Mutt. "Over and out."

"Wahoo!" Wyatt throws up his hands.

Mutt takes a sharp right, and I slam into Veranda's shoulder. She shrieks.

"Sorry," I say.

She glares at me.

"Hey, Mutt," says Wyatt. "What do you do if you come face-to-face with a bear in the woods?"

"You don't run, that's for sure," he answers. "That's an invitation for him to chase ya. Instead, back away slowly. Wave your arms and try to make yourself look big and scary. Make some noise, too—yell or bang a pot. You want him to think you're a threat, but you don't want to block him in. Be sure and give the fella an escape route. The trick is not to get too close in the first place, if you can help it. Tourists see a bear and they want to get closer to take a photo. Bad idea."

His eyes huge, Wyatt takes in every word. The kid is mesmerized. Dinah was right. He IS loving it. I'm glad someone is. We hit our biggest pothole yet, and for a second I think the car is going to flip. It doesn't. My right kneecap hurts from smacking Wyatt's seat, and my stomach isn't too happy either. It's churning like one of those volcanoes you make in science with vinegar and baking soda. I'm probably the only one who hears it, though.

Veranda is staring at me. "Is that noise coming from you?"

"No," I say.

Rose tilts her blond head. "You sure you're okay, Kestrel?"

She knows my name. Breck must have told her.

"Yes," I say, even as I swallow the acid bubbling in the back of my throat.

"You don't look fine. You look positively . . ."

". . . green," says Veranda, looming in for a closer look. *Slurp. Gurgle.*

"That *is* you," says Veranda. "Cut it out."

A cramp slices through my stomach. I groan. "I would if I could, believe me."

"Mutt!" cries Rose. "Carsick passenger back here. You'd better pull over."

"Hurry! She's going to hurl!" yells Veranda.

The second the Land Rover stops, Rose throws open her door. She scrambles out and turns to help me. I barely make it to the bushes before a bacon, lettuce, tomato, and avocado croissant sandwich, two scoops of Gooey Mooey, a waffle cone, and an orange soda burst from the depths of me. It is not a pretty combination.

"Ewwwww," wails Veranda from inside the car.

Once I am done throwing up, Mutt is beside me. His hand is on my shoulder. "You all right, Kestrel?"

"I think so." I lift my head. "Sorry."

"No worries. Puking's nature's way of setting things right."

I look at the ground. "Then I must be one perfect girl."

He chuckles. "It *can* get bumpy, especially in that middle seat." He hands me a bottle of water. "I can take you back to the lodge, if you want."

"No." I stand fully upright. I do feel better. There's nothing left to throw up now, even if I wanted to. "I'll be okay."

"That's the spirit."

As I get back in the Land Rover, I feel a light pat on my back from Rose. By the time we get to the north side of the ridge, the mama bear and her cubs are gone. No one in the SUV says anything, but the air hangs heavy with disappointment. Wyatt crumples into his seat. The photographer starts cleaning his lens. Veranda and Rose stare out their windows. They are all thinking the same thing: *We missed the bears and it is all Kestrel's fault.*

"The afternoon is young, eh? Plenty of other sites to check," says Mutt, winking at me in the rearview mirror. "No worries."

I try to grin.

For the next hour and a half, Mutt drives us up and down and around the mountain over every teeth-chattering, bone-jarring, stomach-sloshing road he knows. We spot a couple of hawks circling overhead, one marmot lounging on a rock (think groundhog), and the tail of a garter snake before it wriggles out of sight.

We do not, however, see a single bear.

7

Dare to Be a Little Braver Today Than Yesterday

Wyatt waves the television remote. "Kestrel, pleeeease, can I—?"

"Yeah." I don't have the energy or the stomach for one more activity today. "But turn it off when you hear Mom coming, or we'll both be in trouble."

The TV clicks on. I shuffle past the sofa toward my room. "Kes?"

"Uh-huh?"

"Don't feel bad," says my brother. "It could have happened to anybody."

"Thanks." It *could* have happened to anybody, but it didn't. I am a walking natural disaster. I should change my name to Hurricane Kestrel. *Oh yeah, I know her,* people at school will say. *She's a Category Five. Whatever you do, stay out of her way.*

"Mutt says he'll take me up with him again when he's got a spare seat," says Wyatt. "For free! You don't have to come."

"Good to know."

My phone is ringing. I fall on my back onto the bed and hold the phone above me. Before I answer the video call, I paste on a grin. "Hi, Langley."

"Hi!" Two faces hover in front of the screen. It's Langley *and* Annabeth.

"How was the lake?" I ask.

"Can't you tell?" asks Langley. "Look closer."

"Is that . . . Is your hair wet?"

"Yes, it is. And *why* is our hair wet, Annabeth?"

Annabeth twirls the damp end of hair around her finger. "Because the first rule of canoeing is never—"

"—stand up in the boat," Langley and I say at the same time, and we all burst out laughing.

"I didn't mean to knock us over," wails Annabeth. "There was this big wasp, and I was trying to swat it away. Before I knew it, we were in the water."

"It's okay." Langley puts an arm around her. "I still love ya."

Annabeth rests her head on Langley's shoulder. I sure do miss them.

"Did you see Aaron?" I ask.

"No, thank goodness," says Langley. "The last thing I need is for him to catch sight of me soaking wet. Can you imagine anything worse than your crush seeing you looking like a complete mess?"

Breck's face flashes in my mind. I have no idea why. Or maybe I do. Breck *did* see me when Mutt dropped us off this afternoon. After being tossed around like a stuffed animal for a couple of hours, not to mention tossing my own stuffing, I must have looked awful. If Breck thought so, he was kind enough not to say it.

"Hi, Breck," cooed Rose when he'd opened her car door.

"Miss Tolliver." He helped her out of the car. "Enjoy your afternoon."

Veranda squealed her irritation quite loudly in my left ear. "What about me?"

Breck rushed around to her side of the car to help her out, as well.

I slid out Rose's door, only to find Breck's outstretched hand waiting. "Miss Adams?"

"You're quick," I said, taking his hand.

"And you're brave," he whispered in my ear as I stepped past him. "Two hours stuck between the Squabble Sisters is medal-worthy."

Unable to wipe the grin off my face, I followed Veranda and Rose toward the lodge entrance. Rose opened the door for her sister. As Veranda waltzed in ahead of her, Rose glanced back and lifted a hand. I figured she was waving at Breck, but when I checked behind me there was nobody there. By the time I'd turned around, the door was swinging shut. She couldn't have been waving at me, could she?

"How is everything in Whistler?" Annabeth is asking.

"Wyatt and I went on a bear tour."

"Fan-tabulous!" cries Langley.

"We didn't see any bears."

Her face falls. "You'll see 'em next time. We'd better go," says Langley. "I promised Dad we'd dry our hair before we go to Dabney's."

They're going to our favorite burger place. Without me.

"Miss you," I say.

"Same here times a million," says Langley.

"Eat some curly cheese fries for me."

"We will," they say. "Bye, Kestrel!"

I hang up. Slipping off the bed, I grab the chair from the little desk, and slide it up to the window. I sit, lean my forearms on the sill, right over left, rest my chin on my arms, and simply look. I scan the trees—hundreds of hunter-green pyramids packed tightly together on the hillside like fans jammed into a rock concert. My eyes travel up to the rugged gray-and-white pinto summit peeking out over the top of the slope, then on to the smattering of popcorn clouds scooting across an azure sky. I could sit here forever.

It's a few minutes before six o'clock. Mom said she'd be back around six thirty and then we'd get dinner. I prop my phone up beside me on the windowsill. I find my contact list, scroll down, and hit DAD. It's a long shot, I know.

"Cole Adams."

"Dad?" Astonished, I sit up. "Hi!"

"Hey, Little Bird. How are things up north?"

"Okay. It's heaven here, except—"

"Glad you're having fun. It was a great place to be a kid— all those creeks, lakes, and trails. I sure do miss the fishing."

"You could come visit."

"How's your grandmother?" he asks, sidestepping me.

"Being brave. I think she's still having a hard time with Grandpa Keith's death. Plus, business isn't so good—"

"Your mom mentioned something about that. Hold on a sec. . . . What do you need, Maura?" I hear rustling and muffled voices. "Sorry, Kestrel," he says. "I'm in the middle of a meeting. We're on a break, so I don't have much time."

"Dad, I think you should come up here—"

"I would if I could. . . . Maura, Welton is going to want that EIS. . . ."

I hear more rustling. More muffled voices. Then silence. My dad cut me off.

I deflate onto the windowsill. A minute later, my phone chimes. It's a text from Dad: Sorry. Didn't mean to hang up on you. Have to get back inside. I'll try to come up on a weekend, okay? Love u.

I text back: Okay. Love u 2.

He's not coming.

Tossing my phone on the bed, I go wash the day away under a warm shower. I dry my hair and get into my denim shorts, rust-colored I LIKE THE SIMPLE THINGS T-shirt, and white, sleeveless hoodie. I put on my socks and shoes, too, because it's almost six thirty and my mother is always punctual. Sure enough, at 6:27, Mom walks through the door to find Wyatt and me in the sitting room—he on the sofa and me in the chair—both quietly reading. She is quite pleased at the sight of us, until she notices Wyatt's sports book is upside down. Busted.

She takes Wyatt's book, turns it right-side up, and puts it back in his hands. "Did you have a good time today?"

"We went on Kodiak Clem's Bear Tour," says Wyatt. "Except our guide was named Mutt. We got to ride off-road in a Land Rover. It was awesome. We didn't see any bears, but we still had fun." Wyatt grins at me.

I grin back.

"Glad to hear it." She rubs her left shoulder blade. "Ready for dinner? Talia is grilling salmon on the patio tonight."

"Salmon!" hoots Wyatt. "Yum."

"Grandma Lark is already down there if you want to go ahead. I'm going to take a shower first. I'll meet you there."

Wyatt zips for the door.

"Mind your manners," Mom calls after him.

We hear a grunt before the door shuts.

Mom glances at me. "Don't you want to go too?"

"I'll wait for you." I'm not that hungry. Besides, I want to get the scoop on what's happening with the lodge. "So, Mom, how did things—?"

There is no point in finishing the question. She is already

heading for her bedroom. My mom does this a lot; chats on the go. If you want to carry on a conversation with her, you have to keep up. I spend most of my life talking to her back. I hurry after her. "Did you go over the books with Grandma Lark's bookkeeper?"

She reaches behind her neck to take off her silver key necklace. I watch the necklace dribble into the little pink decoupage jewelry box I made for her in the third grade. She takes off her earrings, watch, and rings, then, finally, says, "Uh-huh."

I wait for her to continue. Instead, she breezes past me out the door. I stay on her tail as she goes into the bathroom. From the doorway, I watch her take her purple toothbrush out of its clear plastic box. She unscrews the cap from the toothpaste. She carefully squeezes an inch of blue gel onto her toothbrush. Is she going to make me watch her brush her teeth?

"Well?" I press.

She looks at me in the mirror. "We're doing everything we can."

"What does that mean?"

"It's nothing for you to worry about, Kestrel."

Blood roars into my head. "We're doing everything we can? It's nothing for me to worry about? That's what you'd say to Wyatt. I'm not eight years old, Mom."

"I know—"

"Then why won't you tell me the truth? Why are you hiding things?"

"I'm not—"

"You are! At least Breck was honest, and he barely knows me! I don't know why I expected anything would be different here. It's like with Dad." Balling my hands, I spin and charge for the door.

"Little Bird?" She is on my heels. I kind of like being the one chased for a change. "What do you mean it's like with Dad?"

"Never mind," I toss over my shoulder.

"Don't you 'never mind' me, young lady. Wait."

She hates it when I say "never mind." That and "whatever." But sometimes, those are the only words that perfectly describe exactly what you are thinking.

"Kestrel Lark Adams. Hold it right there!"

A few feet from the door, I whirl. "This is exactly what you do at home. You pretend like nothing is wrong when *everything* is wrong."

She flails her hands like I am speaking a foreign language. "What are you talking about?"

"You're always saying things will be better after the next case and Dad will have more time for us after the next trial, but they never are and he never does."

"Calm down, Little Bird—"

"I don't want to calm down, and I'm *not* a little bird. Not anymore. I'm almost thirteen years old! Why can't you see that? Why can't you see what's right in front of you?" I yank open the door, march through it, and pull it behind me as hard as I can.

"Kes—"

The slamming door cuts off my name.

I race down the hall and fly down the split-log staircase. I dash down two flights, leaping over the last couple of steps to land hard on the stone floor in the lobby. Zipping past the front desk, I catch Jess out of the corner of my eye. I smash a palm against one of the heavy oak doors. A sharp pain slices through my wrist. I grit my teeth to keep from crying out. Breck is coming up the front walk, pulling a packed luggage cart with his left hand. I dodge around the cart on his opposite side. I am in no mood to talk to anyone right now. Did he call my name? I don't stop to find out. Running across the flagstone driveway, I turn at the first dirt trail I see. I don't know where it goes. I don't care. I need to get away from here.

The dirt path is thin, and I have to put up my elbows to fight off the branches that grab for my clothes and smack my knees and shins. I run hard, until everything on both sides of me becomes a blur, until the greens and browns of the forest blend like watercolor paints, until all I can hear is the sound of my own breath coming in rapid, sharp puffs. I run for a long time, maybe a mile, maybe more. I stop only when my legs can't take another step. I fall forward at the waist, clutch my knees for support, and gobble air. My lungs ache, but my heart hurts worse.

I don't get it. If she isn't going to include me in anything, why did she even bring me? The answer smacks me harder than the twigs and branches that scraped up my legs.

Because she had to.

Dad's too busy working, and she didn't think I was responsible enough to look after Wyatt, or myself, for the summer. That's the problem, isn't it? I am never smart enough, old enough, or trustworthy enough for her.

Several minutes later, once I can breathe normally again, I straighten. I do a slow circle to take in my surroundings. I see a drooping pine-like tree with bright red berries, a tangle of blackberry bushes, and a thirty-foot section of a tree that's fallen across the path. The rotting wood is green with mosses and lichens. I don't see any trail markers; shoot, I barely see a trail.

I am in the middle of the woods. I am alone. And it's getting dark.

8

Don't Run When You're Angry, Hungry, or Facing Down a Wild Animal

I pat the pockets of my hoodie. Dang! No phone. It must be still on my bed. It had better be. If I lost it I'm going to be in big trouble—if I survive. I try not to panic. I scuff at the ground, pushing aside leaves and twigs to find the squiggly line of dirt that is the trail. All I have to do is follow it and it will lead me back to the parking lot of the lodge, right? Unless I took a turn, which I don't think I did, but I might have. . . . Did I?

The sun is dipping between the trees, casting gangly shadows across the forest floor. I need to get going. I start briskly walking back the way I think I came. My shins and forearms sting from all the scratches. Licking my dry lips, I try not to think about water. Or icy-cold apple juice. Or the sweet, tangy fizz of orange soda—

My stomach rumbles. "Oh, *now* you're hungry?" I say out loud.

As I walk, my eyes scan ahead for something familiar. Yet, each time I go over a small hill or take a bend it's more of the same. More trail. More trees. How far *did* I run? I hope I don't step on a snake or stumble into poison oak. Not that I even know what poison oak looks like.

I've reached a T in the trail. I stop. Did I come from the right or left? The trees look thicker to the left, but the path looks thinner to the right. I want to go left, but I'm usually wrong when I follow my gut, so I should turn right. The breeze ruffles my hair, reminding me I am wasting time.

I choose left. I pick up the pace and get into a comfortable rhythm. After a while, I realize I am singing the new Caden Christopher song. It helps. I'm not thinking quite so much about my growling stomach, raw throat, and burning arms. "Still hanging by a thread from your heart. You kept me on a string from the start. If only you would untie the knot, we could both be free. We could both be free."

I like Caden's lyrics. I'm glad Langley told me he wrote the words, as well as the music. I write poetry. A little. I won a school district poetry contest last year. I got a nice gold medal and a $100 gift certificate to Clarice's Books. It was the first thing I've ever won in my life that wasn't some kind of drawing or random contest. I earned it.

Singing is helping. I don't feel on the edge of panic anymore. Breck is right. Distraction can work wonders. I start in on the third verse and swing my arms to the song. As I hit the chorus, I spot something ahead. It's about twenty yards away on the right side of the trail. It's kind of big. And roundish. And black.

It's a bear!

My knees start to crumble. I grab the nearest tree and drag myself behind it. It's a leafy tree—an alder, I think, and, like me, kind of puny. The slim, rough trunk barely hides me. I hug it. Tightly. My pulse is racing. My brain, too. What do I do? *What do I do?*

I hear Mutt's voice. *You don't run, that's for sure.*

No need to worry there. I'm not sure these legs could hold me up, let alone take me anywhere. Maybe if I sit tight, the bear will move first. I decide to stay where I am. I remain a statue for what feels like forever but is probably less than ten minutes. Finally, I dare to move my head a few inches to peek around the tree. The bear is still huddled on the trail. He hasn't moved. Not an inch. Maybe he's asleep. Or dead. Or playing dead, while he waits out the fresh, young human dinner clinging to a tree. Wyatt will never believe this, not in a million trillion years. I hope I live to tell him about it.

What else did Mutt say? Something about waving your arms to look big. Oh, and making noise to be a threat. I am the shortest girl in my class and lighter than a fawn, according to Langley, who ought to know because she volunteers at a wildlife rehab center. I've never been a threat to anybody or anything in my life. EVER. I glance up. The light is fading. A mosquito the size of a sparrow lands on my cheek. I slap it away. I feel a tickle on the back of my knee. Another mosquito. I swat at it. One way or another I am going to get eaten alive out here. *I have to do something.*

Reluctantly, I release my death grip on the tree. I take one step back. Then another. My heart is slamming against my ribs. Carefully, I step through the underbrush until I am back to the trail. I don't snap even a single twig. Reaching back, I grab the back hem of my hoodie with both hands. I pull the back of my jacket up and out, stretching my arms above my head to make myself look larger than I truly am. I know I look ridiculous. Maybe he will think I am a polar bear. Yeah. Right. I take a deep breath. Then another. On the count of three I will walk quickly and confidently down the left side of the path. I will be big. I will be loud. Who am I kidding? What I will *be* is bear food.

I can't do this. I *have* to do this. I'm ready. Let's start the countdown.

Three . . .

Two . . .

One . . .

Go!

"Bear, bear, bear!" I shout, marching down the left side of the trail. I want to be sure I give him an escape route, the way Mutt said. Yet, he doesn't move. My heart is beating so fast I am sure it will burst. Every shred of DNA in me is telling me to run in the opposite direction, but I tighten my fists and my resolve. Wyatt is right. The fear won't kill me, but the bear might. I can't give in. If I run, the bear will give chase. I've *got* to keep going. "Bear, bear, bear!" I yell again, but it comes out at about half the level of my first cry. Oh, no! My throat is closing off. I'm about ten yards away from the animal now. I can see he's long. And smooth. A hairless bear? Weird.

"Bear, bear, bear." My voice is barely a croak now.

He isn't moving. Something's wrong. Maybe he *is* dead.

Is that . . . ?

I move closer.

What the . . . ?

Just a hair closer.

I drop my arms. I can't believe it. I cannot believe all this time I've been terrified of a big, black plastic *pipe*!

Throwing my head back, I let out a crazy laugh. Doesn't it figure? Langley will love this!

I zip up my hood and turn toward the trail. Wait.

A pipe in the middle of the forest? It has to go somewhere, right?

I spin back. The plastic tube is three to four feet wide, with the bottom third anchored in the ground. It must be old or broken, because the side facing the trail is open and being supported by short, wooden stakes. It looks like a smaller version of a half-pipe used for snowboarding, only turned on its side. It stretches farther than I can see, paralleling the trail for about thirty feet then curving sharply to the right. Following it might lead me to civilization before the sun sets. On the other hand, it might lead me deeper into the forest. I stare at the trail, then the pipe, then the trail again. Why, oh, why did I quit Girl Scouts in the fifth grade? I decide to follow the pipe. It is a decision I regret minutes after I make it because it takes me into a thicket of blackberry bushes. Like witch fingers, the thorns grab at my arms, my legs, my hair, even my socks. Wrestling with the bushes is starting to wear me out. I see a gap in the brambles and leap through it.

Everything on my body freezes, except my eyes. I feel like Alice in Wonderland in reverse. I am in a park. A real honest-to-goodness park with a lake, a small wading beach, a picnic shelter, a concrete walking path, and bathrooms. Is this a mirage? A hunger hallucination? I take a few steps.

Ka-ching! Ka-ching, ching!

I lean back a fraction of a second before a bike whizzes past. It's real, all right. On this side of the bushes, the half-pipe is protected behind thick, black netting.

"You're early!" A man is walking toward me. I recognize the olive outfit, dress socks, and hiking boots. It's the same man Wyatt and I saw in the dining room of the lodge at lunch. "*Bufo boreas*, eh?"

Is he speaking French? We're a long way from Quebec.

"*Oui?*" I say, because the only French word I know is "yes."

"Naturally, you've come to see the western toads migrate,"

he says in perfect English, thank goodness. "Why else would you be looking over the amphibian fence?"

The pipe is a fence? For toads?

"It'll be a couple of weeks yet before they come out of the water," he says.

"O . . . okay." I still don't get why toads need a fence.

He gazes up at the deep violet sky. "I'd better get my students before the park closes."

"You're a teacher, then?"

"Professor," he corrects. "I teach herpetology ecology and conservation at the University of British Columbia in Vancouver." He puts out a hand. "Dr. Jerome Musgraves."

I shake it. "Kestrel Adams. I'm here from Seattle for the summer. My grandmother owns Blackcomb Creek Lodge."

"That's where I'm—we're—staying."

I confess to seeing him at lunch today.

"I met your grandmother when we checked in," he says. "Very nice lady. Her whole staff is top-notch. Everyone is so warm, helpful, and efficient."

"You sound like a commercial."

"I suppose I do, but you can't say that about too many places these days, eh? Customer service is a dying art."

If only he knew how close to the truth he was. . . .

"Have a good night, Kestrel." He turns to go.

"Dr. Musgraves, could I ask you one other thing?"

"Ask away."

"Uh . . . where exactly *is* the lodge from here?"

"Still getting your bearings, huh?"

I nod.

"I am pleased to inform you that you are, most appropriately, at Lost Lake."

I laugh. Not only because it's funny, but also because I am relieved. If I am at Lost Lake, I can't be far from home. I remember the trail marker on the way to the village. Dr. Musgraves offers to show me the way back, but we have to pick up his students first. We head across the beach, walking perpendicular to the amphibian fence, which curves to follow a split-rail fence. It runs all the way to the water's edge. Soon, three young adults come into view. Two girls and a boy are kneeling next to a low footbridge, hammering stakes into place.

"Kestrel, these are my students: Zak Winters, Elise Kim, and Cassie Alvarez."

"Hi," I say. "Is this for the toads too?"

"Yep," says Zak. "The fisheries conservation group and the city built the underpass. Now we're helping to finish the job by adding protective netting and signs."

"I know this is a dumb question," I say, "but why do toads need an underpass?"

"Not dumb at all," says Cassie. "This used to be a standard walking path, so when the toads started on their migration route from the lake to the forest, they'd get crushed by all the joggers, walkers, and bikers. Imagine thirty-five thousand toads trying to cross these busy trails."

I am. "Ew!"

"Exactly. There's another underpass that goes beneath the main road out front. The underpasses should help more of them survive. Western toads are a blue-listed species."

"Blue-listed?"

"It means they're at risk and we need to pay closer attention to how human activities are impacting their populations," says Zak.

"Once the juveniles hop out of the water, we'll start collecting data on their migration patterns," explains Elise. "We'll track as many as we can as far as we can."

"It'll be groundbreaking work. No one's ever done that in this area before," says Dr. Musgraves. "It'll be fascinating to see where and how far into the forest they go. All right, gang. Let's pack it in for the night."

Once the students gather their gear, we cross the field and start up the trail. We reach the parking lot of the lodge as the last peachy glow of daylight slips behind the mountain.

"Good luck with the toads," I say to the professor and his students in the lobby.

"Be sure to come back down to the lake once the migration starts," says Dr. Musgraves. "You won't be disappointed."

I hurry out to the patio, a semicircular courtyard lined with cedar planters, each one bursting with red and white geraniums. The mosaic limestone patio has about fifteen round cedar tables, though all but one is empty. A couple about my parents' age is sipping wine, their faces lit from beneath by the citronella candle in a Mason jar. Behind them sits a large metal grill. It isn't smoking. I missed it. I missed the salmon.

"Your mother's been looking for you," says a soft voice.

"Hi, Grandma." I comb my hair with my fingers. "I . . . uh . . . went for a run. I forgot my phone." My grandmother reaches into the pocket of her black jacket and pulls out her phone. It's no secret who she's calling. "She's here," she says. "Uh-huh. Okay. Okay. Right."

My mother is telling my grandmother to make sure I get something to eat and to come up and get a coat if I am cold and all the other things you say about kids you don't think are capable of taking care of themselves.

After another few "okays," my grandmother ends the call. She turns to me. "Hungry?"

"A little," I lie. I'm so hungry even the geraniums look appetizing.

"Grab a seat. I'll be right back." She heads inside.

I choose a table on the outside edge of the semicircle that sits under a string of round paper lanterns. Grandma Lark returns in a few minutes with a glass of lemonade and a plate of salmon, watermelon slices, and a salad. She places the plate in front of me. "I had Talia heat up the salmon. I hope it's not overdone."

I can't answer because I am busy chugging lemonade. I drink almost the entire glass in four gulps. Ahhhh! While I dig into the peachy-pink fish, Grandma Lark refills my lemonade then takes a seat beside me. She doesn't say a word. The salmon is lukewarm, yet still moist and flaky. I let each piece of watermelon slide slowly around in my mouth, enjoying the cold, juicy sweetness. I finish every bit on my plate. Dabbing my lips with my napkin, I sit back. Grandma Lark is glancing up, so I look up too.

"Whoa!" I sound like Wyatt, but I can't help myself. It's as if heaven has spilled a shaker of salt across the cobalt sky. "So. Many. Stars."

"It's quite a show once you get away from the city lights."

She points to the southwest. "There's Arcturus. And to the east, Vega. They're summer's brightest stars."

I turn to find one glittering star, then the other. "They're so bright!"

"Forty-two years and I never get tired of stargazing from here."

I drop my head. "You've lived here forty-two years?"

"Mmm-hmm. Grandpa Keith and I bought this land when we got married. The only thing on it at the time was an old hunting cabin. We cleared the land and built the lodge ourselves. Log by log. Stone by stone. Much of it is recycled materials from cabins and old buildings. We wanted to make as little impact on the natural surroundings as possible."

"I like that idea."

"Keith used to say it was important to live in harmony with nature, not to beat it into submission. It took us a lot longer to do it that way, but"—her eyes lovingly wander up the side of the building—"there's no hurry when you're breathing life into a dream."

"Dad said it was a great place to be a kid. I can't imagine why he'd ever want to leave."

"He didn't," she says. "Not at first, anyway. After he graduated from high school, he stayed to help run the lodge, but we could tell his heart wasn't in it. Cole wanted to go to college, but he was worried about leaving us on our own. Also, I think he was a bit frightened of the unknown. Your dad was always hesitant to try new things, even though time and time again he'd proven he could do whatever he set out to do. You know that Eleanor Roosevelt quote?"

I shake my head.

"'Do one thing every day that scares you.'" She leans forward, the low-burning candle in the Mason jar giving her chin a buttery glow. "This was *our* business. *Our* dream. Not your dad's. It wasn't his passion, and we could see that. So we pushed him out of the nest. We might have pushed a little too hard, especially your grandfather. Words were said, feelings were hurt . . . then we made the worst mistake ever."

"What's that?"

"We let too much time pass before we spoke again.

You know how people say time heals all wounds? They're wrong." Her tone is suddenly sharp. "Time heals nothing. If the wound isn't closed, time only makes it worse. It leads to infection. Your grandfather and your dad couldn't seem to heal things. I tried to help, but . . ."

So it *was* more than work that was keeping Dad at home. I knew it.

"You should talk to Dad, Grandma, and tell him you want to start over. You can't hide from each other forever."

"That's good advice. For all of us."

I know what she means. I start to play with the corner of my napkin.

She tips her head. "You want to tell me about it?"

"I got in a fight with Mom tonight."

"I figured."

"She can't . . . She gets me so . . . Sometimes I want to . . . What? Why are you laughing?"

"I'm sorry." She puts a hand to her mouth. "I'm not laughing at you. Honest. It's that you reminded me of how I used to feel about my mother when I was your age."

I give her a doubting look.

She takes the challenge. "You think she doesn't have faith in you. You think she'll never see you as anything other than a little girl. You think she doesn't take you seriously. You get so frustrated you can't even finish a sentence."

Yes, yes, yes, and *yes*!

"She treats me like . . . She acts as if . . . She won't even . . . arggh!" My forehead hits the table.

"Try to be patient," says Grandma Lark, rubbing my shoulder. "You're her oldest. She's new at this tween stuff."

I groan. "So am I."

"Give it some time. She's got some growing to do."

I glance up. "Don't you mean, *I* have some growing to do?"

"Nope."

I giggle at that.

"You want some dessert?"

"No, thanks. I'm full."

"It's double chocolate mousse pie."

Double chocolate?

"We could share a slice," she says.

That *does* sound good. "Okay," I say. "Maybe a tiny one."

She goes inside and returns with a slice of chocolate pie that's at least a foot tall! We dive in with our forks.

"This is pure bliss," I say, letting the decadent chocolate melt in my mouth.

"Talia is the best baker in town," says my grandma. "Although it probably helps that I've never met a chocolate I didn't like."

I snicker. "Me either."

As we take turns devouring Talia's decadent pie, I begin to feel better. About myself. My mom. My life. Even though I am not sure what will happen with any of it, I'm glad to be eating pie with my grandmother on the patio under the starry sky. I hope Grandma Lark won't have to close the lodge. I see myself here—years from now. That probably sounds funny, considering I've been here a week, but I do. Some things are meant to be.

Grandma Lark motions for me to take the last bite. I close my eyes so I can focus on nothing but the smooth, rich flavor of chocolate on my tongue. When I open my eyes again, I see a twinkle above my grandmother's head.

It's not a star, though. It's a girl. She is standing on the third-floor balcony. Hand on one hip. Watching us. When she sees she's been spotted, she steps backward, but it's too late. I know that pose. That hair. That diamond bracelet. It's Veranda Tolliver.

9
Dare to Fight for What Matters

I slide my key card through the slot, wait for the green light to flash three times, then open the door. A single light is on in the Alpine Suite. My mom is on the sofa. She is leaning on an elbow, resting on the arm of the couch. Her head is down, her forehead cradled in her hand. I shut the door and her head comes up. Her eyes are red. My brother's bedroom door is open a crack. The light is off.

"I'm sorry, Mom," I say quietly, so I don't wake Wyatt.

"Sorry too." She pats a spot next to her on the sofa.

I sit, folding one leg under me. I latch on to a gold pillow with a cross-stitch of a moose. Hugging it to me, I play with the fringe and wait for the lecture.

"You're right," she says quietly.

"I am?"

"Your dad's schedule is out of balance. He's not home as much as he should be. I'll talk to him about it when we get back, but I don't know that he will change."

I loop a piece of fringe around my finger.

"But I *can* promise you one thing, Li—Kestrel," she says. "*I* will change. I won't make excuses for him anymore or pretend everything is perfect."

"Thanks." I know my mom is in a tough spot. She doesn't want me to think badly about my dad, so she defends his behavior, but that makes me mad at *her*, too.

"I'm also sorry if you thought I was patronizing you by not telling you about the lodge's financial situation," she says. "I didn't mean to do that. It's only that . . . well, I had special plans for you this summer."

"Special plans?"

"Yes, I wanted you to focus on getting to know your grandmother, not worry about business."

"Can't I do both?"

She nods. "I suppose you can. You are quite a capable girl."

Whoa! I am almost certain that is the first compliment she's given me here.

"Besides, Mom, I *am* getting to know her," I say. "And I am learning how much this place means to her." I am also discovering how much it's starting to mean to me.

She rubs her forehead slowly, with two fingers, the way you do when you don't know what to do.

"I won't tell anybody the things you tell me," I say. "You can trust me, Mom."

"I know that. You're the one person around here besides your grandmother I am absolutely certain I can trust."

"There must be others, too," I say. "What about Dinah and Jess? Nita and Madeline? Breck and his mom?"

She is shaking her head at every name I mention.

"What's the matter?" I ask.

"It's possible Dinah's computer was hacked. It's also

possible someone who works here leaked the guest list. That same someone could be behind the bad reviews, too. We have to consider the possibility that one of Lark's employees is sabotaging her business."

"Sabotage? I can't believe Dinah or Jess would do anything like that."

"I don't want to believe it either."

"But why—?"

"I don't know, but until we do we can't trust anyone."

I wonder about Breck. He seems nice, but maybe he's trying to learn information from me to use against my grandmother.

"You asked me how the books are. The truth is"—her eyes probe mine—"I think you already know, but I'll tell you anyway: Business is way down. If things don't pick up in the next few months, Grandma Lark will have to close the lodge."

I was hoping Breck was wrong. "We can't let that happen," I say. "We have to save this place, Mom—we *have* to."

"Li—Kestrel, I'm doing everything I can."

"I know. I want to help too. Please let me."

She nods.

"That means you can't keep things from me," I say. "I want to know the truth, even if it's bad."

Mom gives me a slight grin. "All right."

"Promise?"

"Promise."

I am holding her to that. We are a team now.

"You can call me Little Bird again," I say. "I was mad before. It's okay."

"You're sure?"

"If you don't, you'll be calling me Li—Kestrel forever. Besides, I would kind of miss it if you stopped."

She taps my knee. "Let's get some sleep. It's been a long day and we have a lot of work ahead of us."

Mom goes to close the drapes. I bolt the door.

"Oh, before you go to bed," says my mother, "there is one more thing."

"Yeah?" She has a mission for me! I can hardly wait.

"You're grounded."

"What?"

"You know the rule. You always tell me where you'll be going and when you'll be back. It doesn't change because we're in another country."

"Mooooom!"

"I know you were upset when you stormed out of here, but after you calmed down you should have called me."

"But . . . but . . ." If I tell her I forgot my phone and that I was lost in the woods, she'll barricade me in the lodge for the rest of the summer. She ought to be grateful I'm alive. I could have gotten strangled by blackberries or eaten by mutant mosquitoes or attacked by a bear. This is so wrong! I am about to tell her all of this when I hear my grandmother's voice in my head.

Be patient with your mom.

"Fine," I grumble. "How long?"

"Three days."

"Three days!"

She has that You want to argue and make it four? expression, and since I do not want to make it four days, I shut up.

Great. Grounding means no electronics, so I have to give up my laptop and cell phone. Before I turn in all of my stuff, I text Annabeth and Langley to tell them about my totally unjustified and completely unfair punishment. But the truth? It's not so bad. There will be plenty to do around here trying to save this place. Plus, do I want to know how much fun my friends are having at home without me? This will be the best grounding of my life. Not that I'm going to tell my mother that.

This is the worst grounding of my life!

I toss another shriveled-up geranium into the bucket. This has to be dead flower one billion and one. I've been clipping for almost two hours! This place has too many geraniums. I'm tired. I'm hungry. I'm hot. Worse, I have no clue *how* hot, because Canada uses the Celsius scale instead of Fahrenheit. It's 32° C. If you're American, that sounds nice and comfortable. It's not. Breck says it's around 92° F. I wipe the sweat for my forehead with my side of my garden glove and drag my bucket to the next planter. It's all I can do not to jump into the swimming pool next to me. Ahhhhh!

Two days ago, Mom and Grandma Lark gave me "a few chores" to do around the hotel as part of my grounding. A few? I have been slaving ever since. I dried three dozen glasses for Breck's mom (and broke only one). I completely reorganized the brochure rack in the lobby for Jess. I cleaned all seventy-two slots, which meant dumping out several small dead spiders and one large live one. Eeek! I restocked the housekeeping carts with soap and shampoo for Nita, the head housekeeper, not to mention scrubbing fifteen of the twenty-eight toilets in this place. Thank goodness my grounding ends tonight. I'd never survive another day. Running a lodge is not as glamorous as it sounds!

"Hi, Kestrel."

Sitting back on my ankles, I push up my blue baseball cap. The sun is in a full eclipse behind Rose's head.

"Hi," I say, squinting.

She looks cool in a white one-piece halter swimsuit. A matching sarong skirt ties at the hip. Rose is juggling a towel, a water bottle, and a cream tote bag with an embroidered gold beaver inside a red circle.

She tips her head. "I'm Rose, you know."

"I know."

"You do? Most people confuse the two of us. How did you know?"

"Uh . . ." I didn't think she was going to quiz me! "Let's see . . . For starters, your bangs are a little longer than hers. You also stand differently. Your voice is a little lower than your sister's." And *a lot* more friendly, I want to add. "Oh, and white is your favorite color. Veranda wears mostly pink and red."

"Wow!" Rose holds out her water bottle. "Here. You look hot."

"I'm okay,—"

"I haven't opened it." She thrusts the bottle into my hand, and the jolt of the icy chill against my swollen fingers gives me a surge of energy.

"Thanks." I open it and take a big, long drink.

She starts rummaging in her beaver bag. "Somewhere

in here I've got some sunblock, too, if you need another coat—"

"Stop bothering the gardener, Rose," drawls Veranda. She breezes past in a scarlet-red bikini, a red floppy hat, and red sandals.

"She's not the—"

Eeee-rrk! Veranda is sliding a chaise lounge closer to the pool. "Come *on*, Rose."

"Bye, Kestrel." Rose scurries after her sister.

The more I get to know the Tolliver twins, the more differences I see between them. Rose must know it too. I hope she finds the courage to step out of Veranda's shadow. She deserves to walk in the sun.

I go back to deadheading geraniums, but keep sneaking glimpses of the Tolliver girls. Not that they are doing anything special. Veranda is lying in the sun with her sunglasses on and her earbuds in, tapping her red toes against the edge of the lounger. Rose is reading and sneaking glimpses of me over her book.

"Oh, waitress!" Veranda snaps her fingers at Madeline,

who is walking through the pool collecting empty glasses and dishes. "I'd like a Lemon Fizz soda."

"Lemon Fizz? I'm sorry, we don't have that," says Madeline, balancing a tray of dishes on her shoulder. "But I can get you—"

"You do so have it," clips Veranda.

Madeline adds another glass to her full tray. "I'm sure it's discontinued, so you're not likely to find it anywhere around here. I'd be happy to bring you some of Talia's homemade lemonade, instead—"

"It *is* discontinued, but my dad knows the owner, and they make it for *me*." Flinging her arm out in front of her, Veranda twists her wrist this way and that, admiring the way the zillions of diamonds in her gold bracelet shimmer in the sun. The bracelet catches the light, sending a blinding beam directly into my eyes. "Daddy had it flown in special on his corporate jet. It's in your fridge."

"It is? I didn't know."

"Now you do," says Veranda, as Madeline rushes to obey her command. She flutters her hand like a queen commanding her royal subject. "Don't forget. It'll always be there once we own this place."

I am still blinking spots away when Veranda's words sink in. Dropping the water bottle, I hop to my feet. "What do you mean, once you own this place?"

"We're going to buy the lodge." Veranda wiggles her toenails, painted the exact same shade of red as her sandals. "Why else do you think we're staying here?"

"I . . . I . . ."

Truth is, I had never given it much thought.

"The Fairmont is soooo much nicer but we'll remodel. You have to make the best of whatever situation you're in, right?" Veranda slides her fingertips along the chair rail then shakes them out, as if getting rid of the dirt, even though I can clearly see the chair wasn't dirty. "Somebody once told me that. I forget who it was, though."

I am fuming. She knows perfectly well who said it. I did!

Rose glares at Veranda but doesn't say a word.

I am frozen with shock.

Cory—the lodge landscaper—and my grandmother are

coming this way. "Kestrel, honey," says Grandma Lark, "you didn't have to do *all* of them. I only meant the four planters in front."

I take big strides to close the gap between us. "Are you going to sell this place to the Tollivers?"

"I'm . . . I'm not sure. . . . Maybe."

"Maybe? Are you or aren't you?"

"Kestrel, I don't know. And this isn't the place to discuss it."

"You can't, Grandma!" I shout. "You just can't! This is your dream. How could you sell it to *them*?" I know I sound like a spoiled child throwing a tantrum, but I'm hot and tired and I want to know the truth.

"Come with me." Grandma Lark puts an arm around my shoulder and guides me into the building. When we are inside, and alone, she says, "I know this may be hard for you to understand, but selling to the Tollivers may be my best option."

"But—"

"If I sell, my employees will likely be able to keep their jobs, I'll get a nest egg to retire on, and the lodge will be preserved. The Tollivers have promised to do all the necessary repairs and upgrades I can't afford to do to keep the lodge going," she says. "On the other hand, if I wait and business doesn't improve, the bank will foreclose. My employees will lose their jobs. I will lose my investment. And it will all have been for nothing because the Tollivers, or someone else, will end up buying this place for a song so they can turn it into condos."

She may have a point, but I am still upset. "Do Mom and Dad know you're thinking of selling to *them*?"

"They know I have offers."

"So that's it, then." I yank off my garden gloves. "It's done."

"It's not done. I haven't made a decision about selling yet." She makes me look at her. "But if and when I do, I'm going to need your support."

No! Absolutely not! How could she even ask me that? I cannot imagine her selling this place to anybody, especially not the Terrible Tollivers. It's unthinkable. She is standing there, waiting for me to say something encouraging. I can't do it. The best I can do is dip my head, but I do not mean it. It is a lie. I will never support her selling to them. Never!

"Thanks for your help today," says my grandmother. "Why don't you go on up and shower. It's almost time for you to walk Wyatt back from day camp."

I turn away, then spin back. "Grandma?"

"Yes?"

"Whatever happens, I want you to know something." There is a lump in my throat. "I love it here. I'm so glad we came to visit you. And if I were old enough and rich enough, I'd give you every cent you need to keep it."

Her face softening, she squeezes my arm.

As I walk to the lobby, my hands become fists. I *will* find a way to save the lodge. This is my family heritage and I am not about to let the Terrible Tollivers, the bank, or anyone else take it away.

"Kestrel!"

I crane my neck. This cannot be real. She can't be here. But she is. *She is!*

I swoop toward her. "Langley!"

10

Don't Cheat

hat are you *doing* here?" I screech.

Langley hooks a lock of ginger hair behind her ear. "Your mom called my mom and asked us to come. She said she needed some marketing advice."

"She did?"

"Uh-huh. She said it was your idea."

"She *did*?" It *was* my idea. I didn't realize she'd heard me.

The door to the back office opens. My mom appears. Spotting me, she comes around the front desk. "I see you're in time to greet our newest guests." My mother holds out a white

rectangle to me. My phone! I am confused because, technically, there are still four hours left on my grounding. "Early
release for good behavior," she says quietly, hugging me.

I hug back.

Langley and her mom want to get cleaned up, and I
have to get Wyatt, so we all agree to meet in the dining
room later. Racing upstairs, I take a cool shower and get
dressed. I put on my A-line, buttercup-yellow sundress, and
tan ankle-wrap sandals. Brushing my long hair back, I put
it into a low ponytail and tie it with a yellow elastic band. I
rub sunscreen on my arms and face and add lip gloss before
heading downstairs.

"Hi, Jess and Dinah," I say, on my way past the front desk.

"Hiya, Kestrel," says Jess. He's wearing a green bow tie
with matching suspenders. With his red hair, he looks a bit
like a leprechaun.

"Cute outfit," Dinah says to me.

"Thanks."

"Looks like I'm not the only one that thinks so," she
says gently.

I don't have time to ask her what she means. George is galloping ahead to open the door for me, so I keep going. Flying in from I don't know where, Breck practically body-slams him to get there first. Bowing slightly, he pulls back on the handle of the oak door. "Miss Adams," he says, out of breath.

"Mr. McKinnon," I say.

I skip all the way to Lost Lake, which is strange because I run. I never skip.

"You're late," Wyatt says when I get there. He's perched on a tippy gray picnic table with his chin in his palm, his elbow on his knee, and his feet on the seat.

"Sorry. Langley and her mom showed up out of the blue. How was camp?"

Jumping off the table, he rips his name tag off his shirt. "It stank."

"Wyatt!" A couple of the camp counselors are nearby.

"Well, it did."

"Come on." I pick up his camouflage backpack, and we head across the field. Once we are out of earshot, I ask, "Okay, what happened?"

"Nothing," he mumbles, shoving his hands in the pockets of his shorts.

"Come on, don't be like that. Tell me."

"No, I mean *nothing happened*. All week, I've been waiting for us to do the zip line or go river rafting or have some kind of rippin' adventure. Instead, we sing dumb songs and collect lake water in jars to look at under the microscope. Big whoop. I want to carve a canoe or do archery. Why can't we do fun stuff like that?"

"I'm no expert, but I'm guessing they don't want to give knives and arrows to eight-year-olds."

He grunts.

"It'll get better," I say. "Give it a chance."

Wyatt holds up a red-and-black braided lanyard about a foot long with a flat rock dangling from the end. "I made this."

"That's nice. Um . . . what is it?"

"I don't know."

I laugh. The kid cracks me up sometimes.

"I hate day camp, Kes," he says. "I want to quit."

Mom won't be happy to hear that. She's already paid for

the month. It's not good news for me, either. If Wyatt bails on camp, guess who is going to be stuck babysitting him 24/7 for the rest of the summer?

"We'll talk to Mom," I say in my best big-sister voice, "but—and this is a suggestion—you might want to wait to pack it in until after the toads show up."

"Toads?" His face lights up.

I tell him what I learned from Dr. Musgraves about how the Western toads will migrate from the lake to the forest. I explain how the professor and his students helped with the amphibian fence and underpass to keep the toads safe on their journey. "Want to see the fence?"

"You bet!" cries Wyatt.

We do an about-face. We follow the plastic tube down to the beach, where another barrier—netting held by stakes—has been put up several feet from the backside of the fence, probably to keep the toads in and the people out. I lead the way down to the trail to the underpass. We don't see Dr. Musgraves or his students, but there are some signs up that weren't there before. Tall, bright orange rubber stakes have been driven into the ground—one on each side of the footbridge. Attached to each is a long yellow sticker that reads in bold black letters, TOADS CROSSING.

"Cool!" squeals Wyatt.

"Dr. Musgraves says the toads will be coming out of the water soon. They'll follow the fence up here and go through the underpass and into the woods. I was thinking since you were going to be down here all day you could keep watch and let me know when the toads come on shore." I snap my fingers. "Oh, that's right, you're probably not coming back to camp. Never mind."

He leans out over the footbridge to check out the underpass. "I guess I *could* try it again. I mean, it wasn't completely warped. We did have corn dogs and curly fries for lunch. And I got to see a banana slug crawl over Garth's shoe."

"Okay, but only if you're sure."

Wyatt grunts, which means it's a deal. He isn't going to quit day camp. Crisis averted. For now.

After dinner, I give Langley a tour of the lodge. We stop at the front desk to say hi to Jess, still in his bright green bow tie and suspenders. By her smirk, I can tell Langley is thinking exactly what I was thinking: leprechaun!

"I know what's going through your minds." Jess slides his thumb under one of the suspenders. "How do I fend off the ladies looking so good?"

We laugh. "Jess, this is my friend Langley."

"As in the city?" he teases.

"I could hardly believe it when I saw my name on the freeway sign," says my best friend. "I should have gotten a picture."

I nudge her. "We'll get one on the way home."

As we continue the tour, I tell my best friend that my grandmother may have to sell the lodge. "I'm so sorry," she says, staring up at the arched ceiling. "This place is incredible. It should stay in your family. Try not to lose hope. Our moms will figure out something."

"I'm not sure a new website or a fancy brochure is going to turn business around in two months," I say. "I wish I could figure out a way to make the Terrible Tollivers, and everyone else, who wants to buy this place, go away."

"You mean, like, put a spell on them?"

"I was thinking more along the lines of putting banana slugs in Veranda's bed. Wyatt knows where to get them."

Langley chuckles, until she sees the worry lines on my forehead aren't disappearing. Hooking her elbow through mine, she says, "We'll think of something. Hey, I know. Let's go running tomorrow morning. We've got to get some training in, and I do my best thinking when I run."

Same here. "Okay."

"After that, can we go shopping in the village?"

"Absolutely. You'll love Skitch. It's my favorite store. It has the cutest hand-painted ceramics and canvas prints. Oh, and Cows. You've got to have Cows ice cream."

"Have you taken one of the ski lifts up Blackcomb or Whistler?"

"Um . . . Wyatt has gone up Whistler Mountain with Mom, but . . ." I want to be honest, but how can I tell her I am terrified to set foot inside one of those little boxes of death and travel six thousand feet up? She'll think I'm nothing but a big chicken. And she will be right. ". . . I haven't," I say. "Not yet."

We are at the little library.

"Oh!" gushes Langley. "Great frog lamp. I want one for my room." I knew she'd like it. After a quick look around, she asks, "Is it time for Pick-a-Book Peekaboo?"

As usual, she has read my mind. We've been playing this game since we made it up in the fifth grade. The rules are simple. You pick a book shelf in the library that you don't know very well. You close your eyes tightly (no peeking). You run your finger horizontally across the vertical spines. You can stop any time you wish. You can take as long as you want. But once you open your eyes, you *have* to read the book you're touching; the entire book. I've found some truly epic books this way—books I would never have chosen based on looking at the cover or reading the flap. I've also chosen some yawners, too, but that's the risk you take.

"You first," says Langley.

I decide to go to the farthest of the three freestanding shelves. The small gold sign reads PARANORMAL/HORROR. It's not a genre I usually read. It's perfect. I stand at the end of the shelf and shut my eyes. I slowly slide my index finger across the book. About a dozen books or so in, I pause. *Is this the one?* I run my fingers over it. It's got a thick spine. It's smooth—plastic covering. If I open my eyes, if I choose this book, I have to read it. That's the rule. I'm not yet ready to commit. I keep moving.

"No peeking," says Langley from over my right shoulder.

"I never peek," I say, and it's true. I don't cheat. Ever. Not even if it means getting a better grade. That's not to say I haven't cheated in the past. In sixth grade, Clarissa Bickers let me copy off her test paper in math. I got an A- on the test. The next day I was covered in stress hives from the neck down. I could not stop itching for an entire week. It was the worst seven days of my life. I should have taken the C. Cheating is now permanently on my list of Don'ts.

My fingers stop on a rough texture. A fabric cover?

". . . what's down here?" I hear a woman say.

"Just a dinky library."

My eyes fly open. I'd recognize that sarcastic voice anywhere.

"Hey, Kes!" squeals Langley. "You're not supposed to—"

Grabbing her arm, I pull her into the corner. "Shhh!"

Langley gives me a confused look, but obeys.

"I want a quick look, Veranda." It's Mrs. Tolliver. "Oh my, this is dreadful. Those chairs look like they were upholstered with your father's pajamas."

I can feel my blood start to simmer.

"Hey, a frog lamp," says Veranda. "That's kind of—"

"Hideous," finishes her mom. "Veranda, stand up straight, will you? And why are you wearing that top?"

"I thought you said I could—"

"How many times do I have to tell you, coral is not your color?"

"I don't see why we have to stay here anyway," says Veranda. "I want to stay at the Fairmont. They have that great lounge with all that delish food. Plus, David and Laurel always get me those espresso truffle thingies I like—"

"You know why," says her mother. "Your father wants this deal. We're trying to make a good impression to help push things through."

I nearly snort out loud. A good impression? She's kidding, right?

"The people here are mean," says Veranda.

"Really? I think Jess has proved most helpful, and Dinah is pleasant enough—"

"I meant that girl."

"What girl?"

"You know the one—long, dark hair, always wears those tees with dumb sayings, so tiny I could fit her in my purse."

Raising her eyebrows, Langley points at me. Nodding, I cross my eyes.

"She was on that bear tour Rose dragged me on," Veranda is saying. "She puked all over me."

"I did not puke on her," I hiss. "I puked *near* her. There's a big difference!"

It's Langley's turn to shush me.

"I don't see what Breck sees in her," mumbles Veranda.

Uh-oh! Veranda is on the other side of the shelf! I hope she didn't hear me. I hunch farther down, taking Langley with me.

"I know it's been a less-than-ideal vacation," says Mrs.

Tolliver. "But don't worry. We won't be staying in this . . . this old tree house much longer."

"It is kind of like a tree house, isn't it?" says Veranda, missing her mom's insult. "The wood *is* beautiful. I guess I will be a teeny bit sad to see it go. I mean, I *know* I will."

"Not me," says her mother. "Let's get going. And how many times have I told you, Veranda, to stop dragging your feet? It's quite annoying."

"Hey, Mom, let's get some dessert."

"Dessert? You never want dessert."

"I know, but I hear the chocolate pie is amazing. We could share a slice."

"You know chocolate isn't good for your skin."

"Okay, something else, then. You pick. I've hardly seen you all week—"

"Your father and I are expected at the Ralston's party, and he doesn't like to be late—"

"We'll be quick. Ten minutes."

"Maybe another time. We'd better get going. . . . Will you *please* pick up your feet?"

Langley and I remain still until the swift *clomp* of heels and the scuff of sandals against hardwood fade away.

"Who were they?" asks Langley.

"Veranda Tolliver and her mom."

"You mean—"

"The Terrible Tollivers."

"I wonder what she meant about being sad to see the wood go," says Langley.

"Veranda said something to me about remodeling the place," I say, a shiver going down my spine. "Knowing Veranda, she'll probably want to cover the entire lodge in pink wallpaper."

Shivering, Langley runs her fingers along the edge of a log shelf. "You *cannot* do it, Kestrel. You can't let your grandmother turn this beautiful lodge over to those horrible people."

"I won't," I vow. Now if only I knew *how* to stop her.

Langley is studying me. "Can I ask one more question?"

"Uh-huh."

"What's up with Breck and you?"

11

Dare to Break a Rule (or Two)

I wake up a few minutes before my alarm clock goes off. I am always doing this—opening my eyes right before the alarm sounds. I think it's an instinctive thing. I hate the *beep-beep* noise of alarms, so my brain has found a way around it. Kind of a cool superpower, I think. Kind of a weird quirk, Langley says.

Still, superpower or quirk, I am the one in the lobby at seven thirty on a Saturday morning, ready to go running, and where is my best friend? *Not* here and *not* ready to go running. While I wait, I polish the courtesy apples in the bamboo bowl, straighten the stack of walking maps, and pop off a few dead daisy heads from the bouquet on the front desk. *Come on, Langley! Where are you?*

Dinah comes rushing through the lobby, her skyscraper-high heels rapidly tapping against the mosaic stone floor. She is carrying her floral tote bag, stainless steel travel mug, and black nylon lunch bag. Her face is flushed. A few strands of hair have escaped her perfectly slicked high ponytail. This is not the always-calm, ever-efficient Dinah Sterling I am used to seeing.

I hang on the desk. "What's wrong?"

"Uh . . . nothing . . . nothing's wrong. Running a bit late, that's all."

"But I didn't think your shift started till eight."

She is digging in her bag. "And how are you this fine morning, Kestrel?" she asks in her *I'm asking to be polite, but I don't really want to know* voice.

"Copacetic."

Dinah finds her keys, unlocks the office door, and goes in. Seconds later, she scurries back out. "Forgot my name tag." Back into the office she goes. She steps out. "Argh! My coffee." After the third trip to the office, Dinah finally brakes to a full stop. She exhales and looks at me. "What?"

Still melting on the desk, I look up at her. "You tell me."

"Believe me, I'd love to, but I can't."

I knew it. There *is* something going on.

When she leans to tap the power button on the computer, her sleeve smacks her coffee tumbler.

I catch it before it topples over. "Dinah, slow down."

"It's so unexpected. . . . There's so much to do. . . ."

"For a new guest, you mean?"

Her red lips break into a grin. "It *is* exciting. We've never had anyone so important—"

"Hey!" It's Langley. "Sorry. I overslept." She grabs her right ankle and bends her knee, stretching out her quadriceps. "You ready?"

"As soon as Dinah tells me the secret she is dying to tell me about the important person that's coming."

"Ooooo, a secret VIP!"

"There is no secret VIP," says Dinah, unconvincingly.

I nudge my best friend. Between the two of us, I am positive we can get Dinah to spill it.

"You wouldn't actually be telling us if you gave us a hint," I say. "A teeny tiny hint."

"We could play twenty questions." Langley is catching on. "Is it a girl?"

"Nice try," says the front desk clerk, her professional façade firmly back in place. "My lips are zipped. Go for your run, ladies. I have work to do."

It's a warm, windless morning. Lacy clouds are stretched across the sky like vanilla taffy. We keep to the sidewalk on Painted Cliff Road and follow it toward the village. We run side by side until we meet another jogger coming the other way, then Langley slides in behind me until the other person passes.

"I wonder who's coming to the lodge," Langley huffs.

"Do you think our moms know?" I ask.

"Not mine. My mom doesn't know anybody famous unless you count the news anchor on channel seven—Tabitha Travers. She met her at the grocery store once . . . well, crashed into her cart is more like it."

"I bet Grandma Lark is in the loop. She'll tell me." Stopping, I rest my hands on my knees and gulp air. "Ready to head back?"

Langley is breathing hard too. "Uh-huh."

We back to the lodge, though we have to stop a few times because it's uphill and some of us—okay, both of us—haven't been running as much as we were supposed to this summer. We turn into the driveway of the lodge, shuffling down the center of the cement. Langley's phone is ringing. We slow to a walk so she can answer. It's Annabeth. Langley puts her on speaker.

"Hi, Annabeth!" we say together, huddling around the phone as we walk.

"Hi, guys. I miss you so much," she says.

I know what it's like to be left out. "Me too," I say.

"Me three," says Langley.

Beep, beep!

A black car is creeping up the driveway behind us. Langley and I move to the side to let it pass.

"Whoa!" we say together.

"What is it?" asks Annabeth. "What's going on?"

"You're never gonna believe it," says Langley. "We're right outside Kestrel's grandmother's lodge, and a limousine pulled up."

"No!"

Langley and I look at each other. Dinah's secret VIP!

"She's here!" I say.

"Or he's here!" cries Langley.

"Who's here?" calls Annabeth. "Don't hang up!"

Langley and I take off after the car at full speed. It stops under the entry. Langley and I brake too. Breck is coming out of the lodge, rolling his luggage cart.

"What's going on?" asks Annabeth.

"The car door is opening," Langley whispers, giving Annabeth the play-by-play. "A man is getting out. He's huge. He must be football player. He's dressed in black— black sunglasses, black shirt, black pants. Hold on. Someone is getting out on the other side. Also huge. Also dressed all in black. They are both looking around."

"Bodyguards!" says Annabeth.

"One of the guys is going to the lodge door," Langley says

into the phone. "He's opening it. He's motioning to someone in the car to come on out. He's getting out of the car. It's a man. He's tall, but not as muscular. He's got blond hair. He's facing the other way, so I can't see his face. He's wearing jeans and a red, white, and blue sweatshirt. He's turning this way—no way!"

"What's going on?" cries Annabeth.

"It's *him*!"

"Who?"

"Caden Christopher!" I squeal.

"The singer?" She snorts. "No way. You guys are making this up. Caden Christopher is *not* there."

"He's here, all right," croaks Langley.

"I need proof," says Annabeth. "Snap a pic."

But we can't comply. We can't move. Or think. Or talk. Langley and I can't seem to do anything but gawk as the most popular teen singer in North America bounds past us and into the lodge.

"Kestrel, for the fourth time, you do not need to leave this room."

"But, Mom, I think I lost my . . . uh . . . earring. Yeah, that's it." I slide one dangling silver cat earring out of its hole and into my pocket. "See?" I head for the door. I bet it fell off in the hall. I'll just go check—"

"Halt right there, young lady. Don't think Mrs. Derringer and I don't know what Langley and you are up to. We were twelve once too, you know."

Twirling, I throw a hand to my heart. "Mother, I am shocked!"

"Very nice performance." She is standing near the door to the deck, holding a mug of coffee. "You ought to consider a career in acting."

"Great idea, Mom!" My brain is going full throttle. "I could ask Caden Christopher for advice. You know, he did that movie for the Disney Channel where he was half boy, half robot. I could bop down to his room and see—"

"You will not bop anywhere. Get over here."

I get. Slowly.

"Raise your right hand."

"Mother!"

"Raise it."

I raise it. Slowly.

"Repeat after me. I, Kestrel Lark Adams, do solemnly swear . . ."

"I, Kestrel Lark Adams, do solemnly swear . . ."

"That I will not bother Caden Christopher."

"Is this necessary?"

"I fear it is."

I sigh. "That I will not bother Caden Christopher. Satisfied?"

"And I will not tell *anyone* that he is staying at Blackcomb Creek Lodge."

"We already told Annabeth."

"Besides Annabeth."

"Okay. I will not tell anyone, *besides Annabeth*, that he is staying at Blackcomb Creek Lodge, even though keeping something like this bottled up inside is likely to emotionally scar me for the rest of my life."

She starts to say something but has to dash to the bedroom to answer her ringing phone.

I collapse onto the sofa, grab my phone, and text Langley: Any luck?

She answers: No. Eagle eyes won't let me out of her sight. You?

Same problem.

What are we going to do?

I have an idea, but it's going to take both of us to pull it off. It also means breaking the vow I took thirty seconds ago. Normally, I try to follow the rules, but every now and then you have to bend them a bit. And if the most famous singer in the world doesn't qualify for a rule bend, I don't know what does!

I text Langley back: Let's meet for breakfast. I'll text you when Wyatt is up and we're ready to go.

Mom is back. "I'm going downstairs to meet with Langley's mom. We were up late last night coming up with a marketing plan. We're going with a fresh website, new marketing materials, and a better social media presence. We're also going to contact the lodge's regular guests to give them a special fall and winter rate, plus offer some great deals to everyone else on the website."

I've never seen my mother so animated. I am used to seeing her put chicken in the oven and carry laundry upstairs. She used to be an accountant full-time, then went part-time when I came along and quit altogether after Wyatt was born. I never thought much about her life except to note how it was pinned to mine—you know, taking me to cross-country meets and picking me up from school, that kind of thing.

My mom smiles at me. "And your suggestion about the review thing? We love it. We're going to do that, too."

"Review thing?"

"Remember how you said Annabeth's dad countered a bunch of fake negative reviews about his café with lots of positive ones from trusted customers?"

"Yeah." I didn't realize she was listening.

Mom glances at her watch. "You'll get Wyatt to breakfast and keep an eye on him until lunch?"

"Yep."

"Good girl. I don't know what I'd do without you. Dinah has a list of activities going on in the village. Maybe you can get him interested in something besides video games." She takes a twenty-dollar Canadian bill out of her wallet and hands it to me before leaving.

Once Wyatt is up and dressed, I text Langley and we head down to meet her in the dining room. The elevator door opens on the first floor and we see a packed luggage cart.

"Breck!" I cry. "I wanted to—"

"I know nothing," he says. "And even if I did know something, I couldn't say what that something is."

I follow Wyatt off elevator and watch Breck push his full luggage cart past us. "Oh, come on. Grandma Lark knows she can trust me. Just tell me this: Is he staying on our floor?"

"Sorry, Miss Adams, I am unable to supply that information," he says in his polite bellhop voice. "I don't see what the big deal is," he mumbles, punching a floor button. "I have better hair than he does, and at least I can sing on key—"

The elevator door closes.

Is it me or did Breck sound jealous?

Langley is waiting for us at the entrance to the dining room. As we go through the buffet line, I stay two steps behind my brother to make sure he doesn't drop any sausage, lick any spoons, or drown his Belgian waffle in a gallon of blueberry syrup. Wyatt gets his waffle and goes easy on the syrup. Langley and I get scrambled eggs and toast. I set a glass of apple juice and a little container of strawberry jam on my tray and follow her to a table near the window. Dr. Musgrave's students Cassie and Zak are a few tables down, typing away on their laptops and drinking coffee.

"Wyatt, do you want to do go-karts or the trampoline after breakfast?" I ask.

He grunts.

"You'd better pick one or you're going to be stuck shopping with Langley and me."

"Go-karts."

Langley leans over to me. "How can we find out which room he's in?"

"Front desk computer," I whisper. "If you can distract whoever is on duty, it'll give me time to get into the computer."

"When?"

"This afternoon. Jess goes on duty by himself at four. He'll be easier to distract than Dinah."

"I'm in."

We fist-bump to seal the deal.

A breeze sends my napkin onto the floor. As I am bending to get it, Elise Kim rushes past. "Guys, come on!"

Cassie and Zak slam their laptops shut.

"Let's go, let's go," cries Elise, spinning. "They're here."

I straighten. "Do you mean the toads? They're here? Aren't they early?"

"Yes on all counts!" Elise calls over her shoulder, running for the door.

I start to tell my brother, but he is already out of his seat.

Scooting back my chair, I tap my best friend on the shoulder. "Come on, Lang. We've got to go."

"But breakfast—"

"You can eat anytime. How often do you get to see thirty-five thousand toads!"

"Thirty-five thousand toads?" Langley grabs her toast. "Is that a band?"

12
Don't Step without Looking First

Wyatt, Wait!"

Twenty feet ahead of us on the trail to Lost Lake, Wyatt whirls and throws his arms out in exasperation. "Kessss!"

"I know, I know. Take it easy. We'll get there. The toads aren't going anywhere."

"They are so!"

True, but there's nothing I can do about it. Langley is wearing sandals and has to stop every so often to get the pebbles out of her shoes. She is leaning on me right now so she can take off her left sandal and shake out whatever's in there.

"You go ahead," I yell to Wyatt. *"But keep us in sight!"*

"I will." He won't, but we aren't far from the park.

"So let me get this straight." Langley drops her shoe and slides her foot into it. "These are real toads you're talking about, as in *ribbit-ribbit*?"

"Uh-huh."

"Ick! They're slimy and gross and they have warts, you know."

"They do?" I break into a slow jog.

She falls into step beside me. "Haven't you ever seen one?"

"No."

"Then why in the world do you care?"

"I don't know. Maybe because everyone else cares. I mean, a whole bunch of people went to an awful lot of trouble to build a special fence and an underpass to protect the toads so they could make it to the forest safely. When you see how much it matters to other people, I guess it sort of starts to matter to you, too. Does that make sense?"

"Actually, it does." In a flash, Langley spurts ahead, and I have to pour it on to catch up to her. After a few more turns, the trail delivers us to the parking lot of Lost Lake. We trot past the cars, and I scan the area for my brother. Got him! He's barreling across the open field toward the beach.

"That way!" I call.

Langley has seen him too. We make a beeline for Wyatt, which is easy because we can see his footprints in the dewy grass. Approaching the outer perimeter of the amphibian fence, my brother slows. Then stops. He is standing there, waiting for us, I'm sure. We quickly close the gap. Suddenly, Wyatt's arms shoot straight out from his sides. Whipping around he points at us with both hands. "Kes, stop!"

"What do you mean? The toads are—"

"STOP!"

I freeze. Langley pulls up too.

"Okay, we've stopped," I say, my hands on my hips. "Now what?"

"Look down," he commands.

I do, but all I see is the wind sifting through the long

blades of grass. Why is Wyatt making such a big fuss over—
Whoa! That's not the breeze. It's the ground. It's moving!

"Toads!" I cry.

"Yessireee," says Wyatt proudly.

I bend to get a closer look. I remember Dr. Musgraves described the toads as small, but I had no idea they were going to be positively tiny! I figured they would fit in the palm of my hand, but each one is barely the size of my pinkie fingernail. The toads are the color of wet dirt, their backs covered in shiny, bumpy, light brown warts. Some are jumping, but most are crawling through the damp grass.

"They're supposed to be on the *other* side of the fence," I say, straightening.

Wyatt grunts. "Tell them that."

"Oh, how cuuute," says the same girl who shuddered at their mention five minutes ago. "They are so teeny and bouncy and adorable."

"And everywhere," I say, lifting my foot. "Oh no! I think I squished one."

Langley makes a face. "Icky sticky. You did!"

I feel awful.

Langley goes up on her toes. "Let's get to the concrete, where we can see them better. Everyone, watch where you step."

The three of us carefully pick our way through the grass to reach the gray cement walking path. There are only a few toads on the path, thank goodness. I catch sight of Dr. Musgraves. He's standing on the beach, close to the shoreline where the amphibian fence begins. I inch my way toward him so I don't crush any more toads.

"Good morning!" he says. "I see good news travels—what's the matter?"

I start blubbering. "There's a bunch of them in the field. . . . I stepped on one. . . . It was an accident."

"It's okay, Kestrel."

"We were running. . . . There's no telling how many more we squashed." Tears spring to my eyes. I am a toad murderer! "I'm sorry, Dr. Musgraves. I didn't know they would be that little or that they'd be on this side of the fence," I say. "I should have paid more attention. I should have—"

"It's all right. *Really.* We've all done it. Me included."

"You . . . have?"

"They're so small and there are so many of them, it's bound to happen." He bends toward me. "Okay now?"

I nod, brushing my tears away.

"Come on. Take a look at nature at work. It's quite spectacular."

He is right. We are on the outside of the amphibian fence, the closed side that's protected by netting, but there is still plenty to see. Packs of the miniature toads are leaping, walking, scooting, and crawling up the shore.

"Aren't these guys on the wrong side of the pipe?" I ask.

"They're still safe behind the netting, and most will funnel into the underpass anyway," he answers. "Shall we check and see how it's working?"

"Yes!" I turn to tell my brother to come too, but he has squatted on the sand, his hand reaching out toward a toad. "Wyatt, no! Didn't you see the sign?"

A few feet away, a sign reads SENSITIVE SPECIES: JUVENILE WESTERN TOAD HABITAT. DO NOT TOUCH, CATCH, OR PUT IN A BUCKET.

He draws his hand back. "Sorry."

Dr. Musgraves grins. "I know how hard it is for boys to resist picking up frogs, but in this case, it's the best thing for him and you. The oils and sunscreens on our skin aren't good for the toads, and they secrete a milky toxin to keep predators away that isn't good for us. If you get it in your eyes or mouth, it can sting."

Wyatt stands up. "Gotcha."

Dr. Musgraves, Langley, Wyatt, and I delicately make our way off the beach and down the cement walking path. I count only a dozen or so toads on the pathway and can find only one on the footbridge. He has found a divot in the wood about the size of a quarter and is sitting inside. There's plenty of room for a few of his friends, too, if he wanted to invite them.

I glance at the professor. "Hardly any frogs on the path, at all. That's good, right?"

He gives me a thumbs-up.

Zak, Cassie, and Elise are on the opposite end of the footbridge, huddled near the start of the underpass with their clipboards. We take up position on the other side, where the toads *should* come out before they head on their route into the forest.

"Take a look," says Dr. Musgraves.

Wyatt, Langley, and I kneel side by side on the edge of the wooden planks. I cross my first two fingers on both hands. I hope this works.

I lean out and look under the bridge. Hundreds and hundreds of teeny brown toads are bounding across the sandy dirt toward us. It's quite the traffic jam. It looks like rush hour on the freeway in Seattle, except with frogs instead of cars. Once the toads make it to our side of the bridge, they haphazardly file around the cement supports and continue following the amphibian fence into the forest. The underpass is working! One group comes through, then another and another—they keep coming and coming.

"Look at 'em all," shouts Wyatt. "I wonder if they know each other."

"That's silly, Wyatt," I say. "How would they know each other?"

"It's not all that far-fetched," says Dr. Musgraves. "We think they emit chemicals so they can recognize their brothers and sisters. And since each female lays about twelve thousand eggs, that's a lot of siblings."

"Cool!" says Wyatt. "How far will they go into the woods?"

"A kilometer or two," says the professor. "Many will follow the creek."

"You mean Blackcomb Creek?" I ask. From the bear tour, I know a large section of the creek flows down my grandmother's property.

"That's right," he says. "That's one thing we'll be collecting data on—where and how far they migrate. Some western toad populations have been known to travel up to seven kilometers."

Wyatt looks at me to translate.

I do the math in my head. "About four miles," I say.

"Double cool!" says Wyatt.

"That's a long way to go on such little legs," says Langley.

"It's not a one-way trip, either," says Dr. Musgraves. "They'll dig burrows, hibernate, and return in the spring to breed." Then quietly to me, he says, "But the truth is more than ninety-nine percent of them *won't* come back."

"Why not?"

"Predators, disease, pollution, habitat loss."

"It's a good thing they have people in their corner to look out for them, like you and your students," I say.

"I wish there were more people in that corner with us," he says. "Twenty years ago this was a sleepy ski village. Now it's an international tourist destination. With so much growth and development, the toads are getting crowded out."

"Is anybody doing anything to help them?" asks Langley.

"The conservation group I work with buys land to help preserve toad populations, but the odds aren't in their favor. Humans leave a big footprint."

Another group of toads is coming through the tunnel. One toad stops directly under where I'm perched. He moves his head to the right, then to the left. He puts out one webbed foot as if testing the grass. I bet this is the first time he has ever felt grass. It must be strange to go from swimming in the water to hopping on land. Talk about a complete transformation!

"It's okay," I say. "You can do it."

After a few minutes of getting jostled by the other amphibian commuters, the toad inches his way onto the grass. He takes one hop, then another. The third takes him toward the amphibian fence. He's on his way. Does he know the odds are against him? Probably not. Even if he did know, what would he do? What else? He'd go anyway. It's his destiny. Some things are meant to be.

"Good luck, little guy," I whisper.

~ 13 ~
Dare to Get Involved in Adults' Problems

I am on the leather sofa across from the fireplace in the lobby. My best friend takes a seat beside me. It is two minutes to four.

"Status report," says Langley under her breath.

I lower the mystery I am pretending to read. "Jess is in place. Dinah is packing up. It won't be long now."

We are about to put Operation Locate the Supercute Rock Star into action.

Here's the plan. Once Dinah leaves for the day, Jess will be alone at the front desk. That's Langley's cue to stroll up and start chatting. At some point, she will ask him about Kodiak Clem's Bear Tours. Jess will come out from behind the front desk to get her a brochure from the rack by the front door, but oh, no! All of Clem's flyers are gone. Confession: A half hour ago I slipped them into the storage bench near the elevator when Dinah was busy. Jess will have to go the supply room to get more flyers, and on his way he will discover that—oh, no!—some thoughtless person has spilled orange juice on the floor in the hall (also me). Jess, being the nice guy that he is, will clean up the mess, get the flyers, and come back to find Langley patiently waiting for him and me coolly sitting in this very spot reading. He will never know that his detour to the supply room gave me all the time I needed to sneak behind the desk, glance at the computer, and find Caden's room number. It's an excellent plan, if I do say so myself!

Dinah comes out of the office. She's carrying her floral tote, lunch sack, and travel mug. She says something to Jess, who is checking in a man in a business suit. Dinah crosses the lobby, and out the back door she goes. Once the businessman heads for the elevator, I tug on Langley's sleeve. It's her signal to go.

Hiding behind my book, I keep an eye on my best friend. She plays her part perfectly. She compliments Jess on his buttercup-yellow bow tie then starts asking questions about the bear tours. "Do you really see bears? How long does it last? What does it cost?" Jess patiently answers her questions, then comes out from behind the desk to get her a flyer. Oh, no! The flyers are gone. He tells her he'll be right back and walks down the north hall. The moment he passes me, I'm out of my chair.

"Man the lookout," I remind Langley, scurrying behind the desk. She takes up position in the center of the lobby, where she can see down each hallway and both front and back doors.

Once I'm at the computer, I quickly scan the page tabs: housekeeping, maintenance, back office, front office—there! I click on FRONT OFFICE. A diagram of the lodge comes up, showing the lobby, the dining room, and guest rooms. All I see are room numbers. No names. Oh, no! Am I going to have to click on each room to find out who is staying in it?

There are twenty-eight rooms in the lodge. I don't have time to check every one!

"Did you find it?" hisses Langley.

"Working on it," I hiss back.

"Hurry!"

"I'm going as fast as I can." My hands shaking, I start clicking down the row. Room 101: vacant. Room 102: Samuelson. Room 103: Amori. Room 104: vacant.

Wait! Dinah would never put a celebrity like Christopher Caden in a standard room. He's got to be in a suite. I slide the pointer to each of the suites on the diagram in turn. Cedar Suite: vacant. Pine Suite: Helmholtz. Spruce Suite: vacant. Summit Suite: Tolliver. Alpine Suite: Adams. That's us.

"He's not here!" I say.

"He has to be," she says. "He's probably using a fake name. A lot of famous people do that, you know."

"You know him better than anybody. What name would he use?"

"Um . . . maybe a comic book character? He's into comics. He likes Batman."

"There's no Batman here."

"It wouldn't be Batman, silly. Try Bruce Wayne."

I search. "No, there's nothing—"

"Kestrel, somebody's coming," snaps Langley. "It's Jess. He's coming back!

I see my mistake. There are six suites, and I have only clicked on five. "Just a sec."

"Get. Out. Now!"

"One more sec." I click on Tantalus Suite: Lincoln.

Dang! That's not a comic book character. Is it?

"Kestrel!" snaps Langley. "Go!"

I click the back arrow on the computer. As I fly to the end of the desk, the front door of the lodge opens. It's Breck! If he sees me here, he'll know what I'm up to. I do a 180 and skid back behind the desk, my eyes darting in every direction. There's only one place left to hide. Slipping inside the office, I shut the door. The office is empty, thankfully. That was close! My phone chimes. It's a text from Langley: You okay?

Yeah. What's happening? Why did he come back so soon?

He said he couldn't leave the front desk for that long to clean up the juice. He's calling for someone to clean it up.

So I'm stuck in here?

Afraid so. Stand by. I'll text you when the coast is clear.

Standing by.

She sends a smiley face.

This could take a while. I might as well have a seat. I head for a chair near the door, smacking my elbow on the coatrack. The pole sways and falls forward. I catch it before it clatters to the floor; however, a folder of papers tumbles out of a black leather messenger bag on one of the hooks. Some spy I am! I watch the door, certain Jess is going to come through it any second. He doesn't. Scooping up the pages, I straighten them and place them back in the folder. I am about to close the cover when I notice the top page has a hand-drawn map of Blackcomb Mountain. Did Grandma Lark do this? It's quite good. I see Lost Lake, Blackcomb Creek, and part of the Upper Village. I follow the squiggly blue line of Blackcomb Creek up from the lake so I can find the lodge. . . .

That's weird.

There's a big, rectangular building with a tower where the lodge should be. And is that a golf course next to it? Below the map it says GOLDEN MARMOT HOTEL AND GOLF COMPLEX SITE PLAN. In the corner is a picture of a beaver inside a red circle. What is going on? Is my grandmother planning to remodel the lodge? Where would she get the money? This makes no sense. Even if she *was* planning to renovate, she would never rename it. Goose bumps zip down my arms. There is only one logical explanation for this: my grandmother is going to sell to a developer, who is planning to tear down the lodge and build a hotel and golf course in its place! The lodge isn't going to be repaired or upgraded. It never was. And I bet nobody is going to get to keep their job either. The only thing that *is* going to happen is my grandmother is going to get that nice nest egg she wanted. She lied to me! How could she do that? I need to show this to my mom. I throw the map on the copier, snag a copy, put the original back in the folder, and cram the folder back in my grandmother's bag. I check my phone. Still nothing from Langley. I don't care if I get caught. I've got to get out of here. Slowly, I open the office door.

Jess spins. "Kestrel? What are you—?"

"Hi, Jess," I say, flying out from behind the desk, Langley hops up from the sofa and we meet in the center of the lobby. She sees I am upset. "What's wrong?"

"This." I shake the fist that is clutching the copy of the map. "My grandma is . . ." I stop short. Veranda and Rose are coming down the stairs. I don't want them to hear me.

Veranda is wearing a raspberry-pink satin tee with a short, frothy skirt that looks like cotton candy. Beside her, Rose is in a pale blue tank, white shorts, and white tennis shoes. Over one shoulder, Rose carries the same tote bag she had at the pool the other day: cream linen with an embroidered gold beaver in a red circle.

I uncurl my fist. Straightening the page, my eyes race to the bottom corner to find the gold beaver in a red circle. The logos are identical. No! The Terrible Tollivers are the developers!

Veranda and Rose are gliding down the steps like a couple of beauty pageant contestants.

"Rose!" I call up to her. "Does your family own Golden Marmot Resorts?"

"You don't have to say," spits her sister.

"Yes," says Rose.

"I knew it!" I yell. "You think because you're rich you can do anything you want, but you can't. My family won't let you do it. *I* won't let you."

Rose frowns. "Do what?"

"Go ahead," yells Veranda. "We're not one bit scared."

"Ladies, please," says Jess. "Let's keep our voices down in the lobby."

Sauntering down the last step to stand in front of me, Veranda plants her hands on her hips. We are toe to toe. Her feet are a few sizes bigger than mine, and, with her cork wedge heels, she towers over me by a good six inches. "Nobody, and I mean *nobody* talks to my sister and I that way," she snarls. "You got that . . . I don't know who you are—"

"Then maybe it's time they did." I go up on my toes. "My name is Kestrel Lark Adams, and my family owns this lodge. I may be small, but I don't back down from bullies, no matter how much money they have. And FYI, the word is *me*. Nobody talks to my sister and *me* that way."

"Ohhhh!" Veranda's face is turning three shades darker than her outfit.

Rose bites her lip. "She hates having her grammar corrected."

Out of the corner of my eye, I see Grandma Lark, my mom, and Langley's mom hurrying across the lobby. Jess must have called them.

"Kestrel?" It's Breck. His hand is on my elbow. "What are you doing?"

"Declaring war."

"Are you sure you want to do that?"

I glare at him. "Positive."

Seeing the look of determination in my eyes, he drops my arm and steps back.

"Kestrel, what on earth is going on?" asks my grandmother.

"Grandma, how you could even think of selling our lodge to these . . . these . . . vultures?"

"Little Bird, I thought we discussed this. You said you understood that selling might be the best option—"

"That was before I found out you were lying to me."

"What?"

"You can quit pretending. I found this in your bag." I thrust the map at her. "I know everything. You're going to sell the lodge to the Tollivers so they can demolish it and build a hotel and golf course."

As Grandma Lark studies the map, her mouth drops. "I've never seen this document. Where did you get it?"

"From *your* black leather messenger bag. In *your* office. I didn't mean to see it. I accidentally bumped into the coat-rack and some papers spilled out. . . ." I trail off when I see my grandmother looking past my shoulder. I follow her gaze. She is staring at Jess.

"That's not my bag," she says tightly.

The color is draining from Jess's face. "I . . . I can explain, Lark—"

"Please do," says my grandmother. "Why do you have this design plan?"

"I . . . I . . . Mr. Tolliver . . . I'm supposed to mail it for him."

"Did you look at it? Do you know what they planned to do?"

He nods, but won't look at her.

"You were going to tell me, weren't you?"

"I'm sorry." His voice breaks. "I'm so very sorry, Lark."

I don't understand. Why is Jess apologizing?

"Sorry? What else do you know?" demands my grandmother. "What else have you done?"

Putting a hand to his yellow bow tie, Jess steps backward. He hits the wall.

"Oh, dear," mutters my mother and I think I understand.

Jess has been working for the Tollivers. He has betrayed my grandmother.

"The least you can do, Jess, is be honest with me," says Grandma Lark. "After all Keith and I have done for you—*given* you—over the years, I think I deserve that much, don't you?"

"I never intended for it go so far," says Jess. "I . . . I sold them the guest list, Lark."

I gasp.

"I needed the money and thought it was for when they

were going to take over," says Jess. "I didn't know they were going to call guests and badmouth the lodge. If I would have known . . . "

"And the bad reviews on the travel sites?" asks my mom.

"That wasn't me," says Jess. "Golden Marmot corporate was behind that. I swear, I had nothing to do with it. I told them I would have nothing to do with it."

"So the Tollivers have been behind this from the very beginning," says my mom. "First, they bribed Jess for the guest list so they could spread terrible rumors among your customers and cripple business. Then they posted fake negative reviews online to make sure the cut went even deeper. Finally, knowing you were struggling, they checked in here for the summer to convince you to sell to them, all the time pretending they would keep your employees on and preserve the place when they had no intention of doing either one."

"That's about as cold and calculating as you can get," says Langley's mom.

"You would have been a victim, too," my mother says to

Jess. "Don't you know they would have gotten rid of you, too, in the end? They were just using you."

Jess turns away.

Rose and Veranda start to leave the lobby. "Wait," I say, pointing to Veranda. "In the library, you told your mom you would be sad to see all the beautiful wood go. I thought you were talking about remodeling the lodge, but that's not what you meant, was it? You knew your parents planned to tear down our lodge, didn't you?"

Veranda's glossy pink lips slither up one cheek. She says nothing but admits everything.

As the horrible truth sinks in, nobody says a word. Nobody moves a muscle. No one even takes a breath. Until my grandmother hits the floor.

I walk down ten olive-green tiles, placing my foot in the center of each one. I turn, then walk back. Turn. Repeat. Turn. Repeat. I don't know how long I've been doing this. It feels like forever. Why won't my mother or a nurse or *somebody* come out and tell us what's going on?

"It's long past dinnertime," says Langley's mom, glancing up from her laptop. "Why don't the two of you go the cafeteria."

"Yeah, let's get some yogurt or a slice of pizza," says my best friend. "My mom can text us if there's any news—"

"No, thanks," I say, placing my palms on the back of my hips as I pace. "I'm not hungry."

"It might take your mind off things," says Langley.

"I don't want to take my mind off things." I go back to walking the tiles. Langley gets a bottle of water from the vending machine. Mrs. Derringer goes back to her laptop.

The second my mother turns the corner, I am rushing at her. "Mom?"

"She's okay. They're almost certain it wasn't a heart attack. Stress, most likely. She hasn't been eating or sleeping well since Keith passed, and then with everything else that's been going on . . . anyway, they want to do a few more tests, so she'll probably stay the night."

"It's all my fault," I say. "I shouldn't have accused her of lying to me. I shouldn't have upset her that way—"

"Kestrel, if it hadn't been for you, we might never have found out the truth. Lark might have sold to the Tollivers, thinking they were going to keep their word. And then there's Jess. Nobody saw that coming." My mom touches my arm. "She's asking for you."

"She's not mad?"

"No, hon. She's not mad. Third room on the right. Stay a few minutes, okay? She needs to rest. I'm going to call your dad and check in with Talia. She's looking after Wyatt."

At the threshold of my grandmother's room, I pause. Her head is turned away, toward the window. She is looking at her mountain. There is something peaceful about her—maybe because I have never seen her this still. Streamers of light from the setting sun tint her tousled hair pink and orange. Against the big pillows, my grandmother seems so small and thin.

"Grandma?"

She turns her neck. And smiles. It is her same warm

smile, thank goodness. She reaches for me, tugging on the cord that connects to the machine monitoring her vitals. I scoot a chair next to her bed on the window side and sit down. "Are you all right?"

"Alive and kicking." Her voice is strong. "I got a little light-headed, is all. That'll teach me to skip lunch."

"Do you need something to eat? I can get you—"

"I'm good, sweetie. The nurse brought in some chicken noodle soup, and your mother made sure I ate every last bit."

"I bet she did." I watch the neon green line on the heart rate monitor draw tiny mountains on the black screen. The digital readout on the bottom flashes seventy-two beats per minute. I hope that's good. "Grandma, I am so, so sorry. I should have known you wouldn't lie to me. I got upset when I found the map and then I saw Veranda and she made me—"

"Mad enough to spit fire?"

"Sorry."

"Don't be. It takes a lot of courage to stand up to someone like her. I was proud of you. Not that I could say so— hospitality etiquette and all, you know."

"The customer is always right, even when she's wrong. That's what Dinah says."

"Every rule has its exception," says Grandma Lark. "And in this case, her name is Mrs. Jolina Tolliver. That woman and her daughters have certainly tested the limits of everyone on my staff this summer. She won't eat anything but organic cauliflower and artichokes grown in Quebec, and she must have her $100-a-cup gourmet coffee from Indonesia every morning. Do you know she refused to bathe with anything but towels made by Imperial Turkish Plush? And they had to be Caribbean blue—not aqua, not turquoise, but Caribbean blue. We had the towels, but I couldn't find the color. Then I discovered it's not even available in Canada."

"What did you do?"

"Dinah bought some teal-colored towels at the Walmart in Squamish and Nita sewed in the label."

I snicker. "They didn't."

"They did. She never knew the difference. It was the label she wanted. That's all she cared about." Grandma Lark ruffles her short crop. "I feel sorry for those girls of hers."

"Sorry? For *them*?"

"Haven't you noticed? Mrs. Tolliver orders her daughters around the same way she does her employees. And mine. No wonder Veranda barks at everyone. She's copying her mother."

"Maybe, but she still has a choice. Rose isn't that way. Veranda's the one that's a huge pain in the—"

"Adams?" A nurse flings the curtain aside.

Grandma Lark and I laugh at her timing.

The nurse takes my grandmother's temperature by placing a scanner on her forehead. We wait for the beep. "Ninety-eight-point-eight. Excellent," proclaims the nurse. She bustles out, whipping the privacy curtain back into place with one quick jerk.

"You know, the way you took on Veranda Tolliver today reminded me of Keith," says Grandma Lark. "He wasn't afraid to fight for what was right. You have his spirit, Little Bird."

That makes me feel good. I will never be able to say I truly knew my grandfather, but I *am* learning more about the kind of man he was. I'd like to carry a part of him with me as I go through life. If Grandma Lark is right, maybe I already do.

"Grandpa Keith gave you your nickname, you know," she says.

"Little Bird? He did? I always thought Mom and Dad—"

"No." She smiles. "You were a tiny thing—maybe two months old—when your parents brought you up for a visit. You know how babies tend to cry if anyone besides a parent holds them? Not you. Your grandpa picked you up and you didn't utter a sound. You looked him straight in the eye. Then you tried to put your finger up his nose. He said, 'This little bird has courage, not to mention a good right hook,' and you've been Little Bird ever since."

I had no idea. I'm glad I know the real story.

Grandma Lark's eyes glisten. "Before you came in I was lying here wondering what Keith would say about everything that's happened. I've certainly made a mess of things, haven't I?"

"You haven't," I say. "And I know Grandpa Keith would

agree. There's nothing you could have done. The Tollivers set out to get the lodge, and they used every dirty trick they could think of to do it. Your only mistake was taking them at their word."

"I'm certainly caught in their web now," says my grandmother.

She is right. For all of my brave words to Veranda and Rose, we cannot stop them. Grandma Lark can sell the lodge or lose it to foreclosure, but we both know that one way or the other the Tollivers will win. They *will* buy our property. They *will* destroy our lodge. They *will* build their monster hotel and golf course.

I pick up her left hand. Her fingers are cool. I put my thumb on her wedding band, spinning it slightly so the lapis and turquoise mountains face out. "We'll make the most of the time we have," I say. "We'll remember this summer for the rest of our lives. I promise, Grandma." And like Grandma Keith, I never break a promise.

"I like the sound of that," she says. "A summer to remember."

"I wish we could save the lodge, Grandma. This is your life . . . your dream . . ."

"What a glorious dream it was. It lasted for forty-two years. How many people get to say that? I'm so lucky." She squeezes my hand. "No dream lasts forever. Eventually, we must all wake up."

She has lost so much in such a short time. It's my loss, too. I already miss it—the warm brown log walls, the cozy library, the earthy fragrance of a billion and one geraniums—I miss it all.

I fight back the tears, but one gets away. It slips down my cheek.

"Don't cry, Little Bird," she says softly, reaching up to wipe it away.

I try to stop. I do. But the more I try, the more tears fall.

14
Don't Talk to the Enemy

I t's not even nine a.m., and already my best friend and I have dusted the lobby, polished the front desk, refilled the courtesy apple bowl, straightened the magazines, and scraped gum off the flagstone walkway (ew!). Now we stand side by side in front of Dinah. "What's our next assignment?" I ask.

Dinah grins. "You guys are lifesavers. You know that, don't you?"

We know. Grandma's coming home today. My mom is at the hospital right now, picking her up. Jess is gone. Nobody knows where. I'm sure he knows he is no longer welcome here, but his absence means Dinah is handling everything on her own. Well, not *all* on her own. Langley and I are here.

Dinah straightens a small stack of papers. "The day before guests check out, we give them a copy of their bill so they can review the charges and ensure everything is accurate. You'll see that the room number and the guest name is at the top of each page. All you have to do is quietly slide the page under the appropriate door. . . ."

I can't help noticing Dinah's computer is open to a file that says *Guest List*. How did I miss that when I was snooping around for Caden Christopher's room? I try scanning the list with my right eye, while looking at Dinah with my left eye, which is not easy. Okay, it's pretty much impossible.

Dinah blocks the screen. "Understand?"

"Yes," says Langley.

"Uh . . . yeah, right," I say, uncrossing my eyes.

"And no knocking on doors or bothering anyone to try to find a certain you-know-who." Dinah eyes me. "You're part of the team now, and we give nothing less than top-notch customer service here at Blackcomb Creek Lodge. The safety and welfare of our guests *always* come first."

I sigh. "Okay, Dinah. I get it."

"Remember it, because something tells me one day you'll be running this place."

I snort. "Only if I work for the Tollivers."

Langley and I divide the pages between us. She takes the first floor and the south wing of the second floor, while I take the north wing of the second floor and all of the third floor. I am bending to slide the bill under the door of the Summit Suite when it opens.

I groan.

"Kestrel, hi!" I look up to see Rose in a white gauze peasant blouse and matching gypsy skirt. Her blond hair is twisted into a tight bun on her head, though a few wispy tendrils have been left free to brush her collarbone. A small oval cameo dangles from her neck. Glancing over her shoulder, Rose steps into the hall and shuts the door. "Is your grandmother okay?"

"Yeah." I straighten. "It wasn't a heart attack."

"Thank goodness. I was coming to find you. We're . . . uh . . . leaving today, but I didn't want to go without telling you . . . I mean, I knew my parents wanted to buy the lodge, but I didn't know all of the sneaky things they were doing to get it. Or that they planned to tear it down. I'm sorry. And I'm sorry for the way Veranda treated you."

"You don't have to apologize for her—"

"I'm not. I'm apologizing for myself. I didn't stop her when she said all that mean stuff to you. I should have set a better example. After all, I am the eldest."

"You're older than Veranda?"

"By four and a half minutes," she says. "Look, Kestrel, I know we can never be friends, but I hope you'll accept my apology."

I shake my head. "I don't know, Rose."

She nervously twists her cameo. "Of course. I understand. It's too much to ask—"

"I mean, 'never' is an awfully long time," I say, the corners of my lips turning up.

Her face relaxes. "It is, isn't it? So then . . . we're . . . we're . . ." She is afraid to say it.

"Not enemies?" I offer.

She laughs. "I'll take that. I . . . I hope everything works out for your grandma and the lodge. I mean it."

I believe her.

I say good-bye to Rose and head downstairs for my next assignment. Langley is vacuuming the lobby.

Dinah motions to me. "Kestrel, will you watch the front desk so I can run to the restroom?"

"Uh-huh."

"If anyone calls or needs anything, I'll be back in two minutes. Two minutes."

"I can handle it, Dinah." I put on her phone headset. Standing here in her spot behind the desk makes me feel grown-up. I'm not one bit scared. Okay, I'm a bit scared. I'm new at this. I hope nobody asks me a complicated question.

A delivery guy comes in with a basket of daisies. I have him put it with the other bouquets on the far end of the desk. It's the third floral arrangement this morning. The moment people heard my grandmother had gone to the hospital, the flowers started pouring in. Dinah says Grandma Lark has lots of friends and news travels fast in a small town. Something tells me the flowers are for more than just to wish my grandmother a speedy recovery. Like Dinah says, news travels fast.

The phone is ringing. I'm on! I hit the talk button. "Blackcomb Creek Lodge, front desk. This is Kestrel. How may I help you?"

"I'm sorry. I was trying to reach another room but it won't go through."

It's him. It's Caden Christopher! I'd know that voice anywhere. I wave like crazy to Langley, but she has vacuumed herself into a corner and her back is to me.

"Hello? Are you still there?"

"Yes, yes," I say. "Uh . . . um . . . did you hit the pound key first?"

"I don't think so."

"Hit the pound key then the room number and that should put you through," I say. "If it doesn't, call me back, okay?"

"I will. Thanks."

I start to say he's welcome but he's gone. Caden is gone. I cannot believe that I . . . that he . . . that we . . .

"Excuse me, miss?"

"Yes?" I whirl around. "Dad!"

"Hi, kiddo!"

I start to run around the desk to give him the biggest hug a daughter can give and forget I am wearing a headset with a plug. I drag the whole phone system with me across the front desk.

"Oops!" I say, trying to put everything back.

Dinah meets me at the corner of the desk. "Took me a year to stop doing that," she says. She turns to my father. "Can I help you, sir?"

"Dinah, this is my dad, Cole Adams. Dad, this is Dinah Sterling."

"It's a pleasure to finally meet you, Mr. Adams," she says, and they shake hands. "Your mom is always talking about you. She's so proud of the environmental law work that you do."

Dad grins.

The phone is ringing. "You'd better let me get this one." Dinah takes the headset from me.

"Didn't you talk to Mom?" I ask my dad. "Grandma's okay. It wasn't a heart attack."

"I know, but some things you need to see for yourself," he says. "I should have come up sooner. I didn't realize things had gotten so bad." He shakes his head. "I didn't realize a lot of things until I almost lost Mom. I should have been here for my dad's funeral. You were right, Kestrel, I should have come. I was just . . . just . . ."

I know. And none of it matters anymore. "She'll be happy you're here," I say. "You have a lot to talk about."

Breck is wheeling the luggage cart past with my dad's suitcase. We exchange smiles.

"Kestrel?" It's Dinah. "I could use your help again. Langley's, too."

"I'll let you get back to work," says my dad, with a wink. "I'll catch up with your mom and grandmother at the hospital. See you later, Little Bird."

Once Langley and I are in a huddle with Dinah, she

says, "First, I have to know I can trust you to keep everything I am about to tell you and everything you are about to do top secret."

"You can trust us," I say, as Langley bobs her head.

"I need a favor," says Dinah. "Actually, the favor isn't for me. . . . It's for Caden Christopher."

At the mere mention of his name, Langley and I grab each other and start jumping. We can hardly believe it. Supercute rock star Caden Christopher needs a favor. From us! Hoooooray!

Dinah twists her lips. "Maybe this was a bad idea."

"Sorry, sorry," I say, remembering my vow to be professional and put the guests first. "What does he need?"

"Not here," Dinah says mysteriously. "I'll let your mom take over, Langley."

"My mom?" gulps Langley.

We turn to see Mrs. Derringer standing at the corner near the elevator. She signals for us to come with her. The minute the elevator door closes, Langley swings to her mother. "All right, Mom, what's up?

"Not here," Mrs. Derringer says as mysteriously as Dinah. "In a minute, sweetie."

Ding.

The elevator opens to the second floor. No one says a word. Crossing the catwalk to the south wing, I peer over the rail. Tipping her head, Dinah gives me the tiniest of nods. I return it. I feel like an international spy. Technically, I am one, because, after all, this *is* Canada. Mrs. Derringer leads us to the Tantalus Suite.

"You forgot to say presidents," I whisper to Langley.

"Huh?"

"You said to try comic characters. I should have tried presidents. The guest name in the computer for this suite was Lincoln."

Langley snaps her fingers. "That's not a president. I mean, it *is* a president, but it's also his hometown. Caden's from Lincoln, Nebraska."

Mrs. Derringer knocks on the door three times. He waits a few seconds, then knocks twice. A secret knock! The door unlatches and opens. One of the muscled bodyguards leads us into the sitting room, where two more big guys are lounging.

A balding man in a dress shirt and jeans comes toward us. "Hello. I'm Richard Hoskins, Caden's manager."

"Chandra Derringer," says Langley's mom. "This is my daughter Langley and her friend Kestrel Adams. Kestrel's family owns the lodge."

Langley and I are scanning the room, but there's no sign of Caden. He must be in the bedroom or the bathroom. I wonder if he's as fussy about his towels as Mrs. Tolliver.

"Thank you for agreeing to help," says Mr. Hoskins. "As I explained to Dinah, we need to get Caden through the village and to a private concert today, but, as you know, the streets are pedestrian-only, so driving him is out of the question. With these guys"—he tips his head toward one of the giant bodyguards—"we certainly can't walk him there. He'd be mobbed."

Langley's mom turns to us. "That's where you come in, girls."

I get it. "You want us to walk with Caden through the village?" I ask.

"Exactly," says Mr. Hoskins. "All you have to do is act natural, like normal teenagers on vacation."

"Won't people recognize Caden?" I ask.

"He'll be in disguise. Also, he rarely gets recognized when he's with other kids. Usually, if someone *is* suspicious, by the time they think, *Was that who I thought it was?* he's a block away. People tend to see what they expect to see, and when they see three teens they don't expect one of them to be Caden Christopher. So what do you think? Can you two handle it?"

"Absolutely," I say.

"Yuh-huh," says Langley, but her head is bouncing like crazy and she's got a goofy, lovesick look on her face. I hope she can pull this off. She is already failing the *act natural* directive, and Caden isn't even in the room.

"Don't dawdle, but don't rush," says Mr. Hoskins. "Don't make eye contact with anyone. Don't leave his side. And whatever you do, do not call him Caden."

"What should we call him?" I ask.

"Bob."

Langley and I laugh. Even Mrs. Derringer is grinning.

"Our security team will meet you at the concert site and usher Caden to a secure backstage location," says Mr. Hoskins. "You'll then be free to return here on your own or you're welcome to stay for the concert if you want."

Stay for the concert if we *want*? Is he kidding? We want! We want!

"Yes, we'd like to see the concert," I say calmly.

"I'll meet the girls there and make sure they're comfortable," Mr. Hoskins says to reassure Langley's mom, then to us, "How do front-row seats sound?"

My mouth falls so far I hear a pop in my head. Front-row seats at a private Caden Christopher concert? Langley and I are like shaken soda bottles. One more twist and we're gonna blow!

"Girls, if you run into trouble at any point along the way, call Langley's mom or Dinah at the front desk," directs Mr. Hoskins. "Our team will come to the rescue if things get dicey. Once the concert is over, our security staff will get Caden back here safe and sound. They know how to throw off the fans and photographers. We'll stay the night and head to Vancouver tomorrow."

The bedroom door opens, and a tall young man steps out. I almost don't recognize Caden. He's wearing a shaggy, chestnut brown wig. It's different from his usual wavy blond hair. He's got on a loose white T-shirt with a red Canadian maple leaf emblem on the shoulder and jeans. In his right hand he's holding a towel—nothing special, just one of the regular hotel towels. Nice.

"Caden, this is Kestrel Adams," says Mr. Hoskins. "Her grandmother owns the lodge. This is her friend Langley Derringer, and her mom."

Ice-blue eyes peer straight into my soul. "Good to meet you, Kestrel and Langley. Thanks for helpin' out."

"Hi," we say shyly.

Caden trades his towel for a light blue Vancouver Canucks cap, putting it on over the wig. Honestly, if we passed on the street, I wouldn't give him a second look. If my best friend can keep her googly eyes in her head, this plan might work.

"Everybody ready?" asks Mr. Hoskins. "We all know what to do?"

"Yes," Langley and I say.

Mr. Hoskins hands Caden an envelope. One of the bodyguards opens the door for us.

"Relax. Be yourselves. Have fun." Mr. Hoskins waves. "Off you go."

I take the lead, Caden follows, and Langley brings up the rear. No one is ever going to believe in a million years that I, your ordinary American twelve-year-old, helped a rock star in disguise get to a concert.

"I'll see you up there in about an hour," Mr. Hoskins says to Caden before the door shuts.

Up there?

In the hall, I spin. "Ca—Bob, I thought the concert was in the village."

"No."

My heart is, suddenly, slamming against my ribs. "Then where is it?"

He gives me that magical grin that turns average, ordinary American twelve-year-old girls into syrup. "At the top of Whistler Mountain."

15
Dare to Do the Thing
I Fear Most

Did he say . . . ?

Oh, no. *No!*

I force my quivering legs to get in the elevator with Caden and Langley. What am I going to do? There is no way I can get on the gondola of death.

I have to.

But I can't.

I have to.

But I can't.

My brain is spinning. It's mush. It's spinning mush.

"It's okay," Langley whispers, putting an end to my loop of dread. "You don't have to go with us. I can take him up."

"But we're both supposed to—"

"Nobody has to know. We'll say someone recognized him in the village and you were the decoy. You led the girl away. Wait for me at the base of the mountain. I'll drop him off with his security team and come right back down."

She knows! I start to ask her how she found out about my fear of heights, but she only says, "Later."

"What about the concert?" I hiss.

"I don't want to go without you."

"Oh, Langley. Are you sure?"

"Yes. It'll be fine."

I feel awful. We are going to miss seeing Caden Christopher sing from our *front-row seats*, all because of me!

"Here we go," says Caden, as the elevator opens to the lobby.

Dinah is behind the front desk. "Good morning, kids," she says calmly.

"Morning," I say, raising my eyebrows as we pass.

Langley holds the door open for George, who's coming

behind us pulling a luggage cart crammed with backpacks. "Thanks, guys," he says. He doesn't seem to recognize our famous friend, which is a good sign.

Once outside, I look for Breck but don't see him. The three of us stroll down the tree-lined driveway. I want to ask Caden a million questions, and I can see by the look on Langley's face she does too, but both of us are too shy. We're supposed to talk like normal teenagers, and now we are too starstruck to say a word!

"Soooooo," says Caden, stuffing his hands on his pockets. "You are two of the quietest girls I've ever met."

"Sorry, Bob," I say. "Okay, I have to know. Where did Bob come from?"

He laughs. "I have an angelfish named Bob."

"I didn't know that," says Langley, astonished. "I know everything about you. How did I not know that?"

I shoot Langley a glare that says *Shut up, we don't want him to think we're crazed stalker fans*. She gives me a *sorry* look back.

"Also, Bob Dylan is one of my idols," says Caden. "I

never planned on being a singer. Or being famous, for that matter. All I ever wanted to do was write songs, but put one song on the Internet and suddenly your whole life changes."

"Isn't that what everyone dreams of?" asks Langley.

He lifts a shoulder. "I guess, but I miss my old life. I miss sittin' in the barn and writing songs—you know, playing my guitar and singing to the cows."

"You should take some time off," I say.

He smirks. "If only it were that easy."

We turn onto Painted Cliff Road. The sidewalk is clear, except for an elderly woman walking her poodle on the other side of the street.

"Ca––Bob, you ought to write a song with Kestrel," says Langley. "She won a poetry competition last year."

He turns to me. "Yeah?"

"It was no big deal," I say. "It was a contest held by our public library."

"Her poem was great," says my best friend. "It was about honesty and helping each other. It made me cry, it was so good. You should show it to him, Kes—"

"Langley, he doesn't want to see my dumb—"

"Sure, I do," says Caden. "Great lyrics *are* poetry."

My legs turn to oatmeal.

We take the corner onto Blackcomb Way, and although there are more people here, most are walking or jogging or talking to friends. Nobody is paying any attention to us. This is going to be easier than I thought!

We stop at the intersection of Lorimer and Blackcomb to wait for the light. Langley takes a minute to text her mom that everything is going according to plan. Once we cross the intersection, we'll head through the Upper Village and into the main square. The gondola is at the farthest end of the village.

"So, do you have a favorite place to eat here?" asks Caden. He is talking so he doesn't make eye contact with the people waiting to cross on the other side.

"I'm seriously addicted to Cows ice cream," I say.

"Same here." He laughs. "Wowie Cowie?"

"Gooey Mooey."

"Oh yeah, that one *is* good. Have you ever tried the Udderly Sinful Chocolate?"

"It's on my list."

"Uh . . . guys?" Langley cuts in. "I think we have a problem."

"Where?" I ask.

"Don't look now, but straight ahead."

Naturally, we glance up. On the other side of the cross-walk, three girls are gawking. They look a couple of years younger than me. Each is wearing a different color of pastel shorts: peach, yellow, and pink. They remind me of a trio of Easter eggs. Uh-oh. The Easter-egg girls are waving at us.

Caden looks behind him, pretending he thinks they are waving to someone else. "You're in a disguise," I hiss. "How could they possible know it's you?"

"It's called Cadar," says Langley. "I read it about it in a magazine. No one knows how the girls know. They just do."

"I don't think we should stick around to watch their Cadar zero in," I say. "Come on, Langley and *Bob*." I grab Caden's hand and pull him down the sidewalk. We aren't running, but we sure aren't walking, either.

"It's him! It's Caden!" We can hear the girls yelling, but there are too many cars and they can't cross.

"Let's go, let's go, let's go," I shout.

With Caden and I linked and Langley a few steps behind us, we zip right, then left, then right again. We are dodging pedestrians like loose tires rolling at us in some kind of car-racing video game. Once we are out of sight of the girls, I search for a break in traffic. I'm hoping they'll think we turned right into the aboriginal center to hide, which should give us enough time to sneak through the alleys of the main village and get Caden to the gondola. There's our break!

"Now!" I shout, and the three of us bolt across Blackcomb Way.

We scramble through an alley, take a hard right at the ski shop, and come out at the steps leading to the village. Hurrying down a couple dozen steps, we rush across the covered bridge at Fitzsimmons Creek, follow the walkway into the Upper Village, and take a left to skirt the Pan Pacific hotel. We don't stop until we reach the corner of the hotel.

"I think we lost them," I say, huffing as I glance behind us.

"There it is!" says Langley, also trying to catch her breath. The gondola entrance is less than one hundred yards in front of us. All we have to do is get across the redbrick square.

"Cool and calm, everybody," says Caden, reaching into his back pocket for the envelope with our tickets. "Cool and calm."

The three of us casually saunter across the square. We point at the gondola sailing up the mountain as if we can't wait to get on. But one of us can wait. And *will* wait. I'm not sure when I should tell Caden I won't be going. In front of the roundhouse, fence-like steel barricades are set up in a maze pattern. They funnel the lift line to a gate with two turnstiles. An employee sits at each turnstile, scanning tickets before letting people go through into the roundhouse. There are only about fifteen people ahead of us, so it doesn't take long to snake our way up to the gate. Langley leads us to the left turnstile. Caden is behind her. I bring up the rear. Our ticket taker is a muscular woman who could easily qualify as one of Caden's bodyguards, if she wanted. Sitting on a wooden stool, she holds up her hand to signal for us to wait. I need to tell Caden I'm not going up.

An image flashes in my mind. I see myself standing at

the base of the gondola, watching Caden and Langley glide up the mountain. A thought strikes me like a billion volts of electricity: *THIS is it!* If I don't go now, I never will. If I cannot summon the courage to go with my best friend and my favorite singer to the top of Whistler Mountain and sit in the front row of what will be the most incredible concert of my life, then what *will* it take for me to beat my fear of heights? I can't think of a single thing. And *that* scares me more than anything.

Caden hands a ticket to Langley then turns to give one to me.

"Actually," says Langley. "Kestrel is . . . uh . . . staying behind."

"No," I say, my voice catching. "I'm going."

Her eyes bulge. "You're going?"

I give a weak nod.

Langley pumps her fist. "O-kay!"

The ticket taker motions for us to step through the turnstile.

"Caden Christopher!" The name booms across the square. We've been caught! The crazed trio of Easter-egg fans are sprinting toward us, their little pastel peach, yellow, and pink purses flying out behind them. "Wait for us!" they screech. "Caden, wait!"

Blip. Langley goes through the turnstile.

"Coming through! Coming through!" the girls shout, but while we've been waiting, the line behind us has grown to about forty people, and no one is letting them cut in.

I spin Caden to face the building. "GO!"

Blip. Caden pushes through the turnstile. It's my turn.

Blip. I am moving the big spoke forward when pain slices through my neck. I am being jerked backward. "Ow!" One of the girls has a chunk of my hair. I bet it's the peach chick. She was the loudest and the fastest of the three.

"You're not allowed to jump the line," scolds the ticket taker. "Let go of her."

The girl releases my hair. She points to Caden, who is staring at his feet with his hands in his pockets. "Do you know who that it is?"

"Yeah," says the woman, getting up off her stool. "I know exactly who that is."

I suck in my breath. This cannot be happening. Our cover is about to be blown in the most public place possible!

"He's a guy with a ticket," says the woman. "Do you girls have tickets?"

I exhale.

"No, but—"

"Then you're going to have to buy them at the counter around the corner, and then you're going to have to stand in line like everyone else. Got it?"

"Yes, but—"

"Don't make me call security. Miss?" She beckons to me, and I quickly go through the turnstile. Caden, Langley, and I rush for the platform. The next car is ours.

"This is going to be fun," Caden says for the benefit of the guy who is helping everyone get on.

"I bet the view is great," says Langley, her face pale.

Our gondola car makes a slow 180-degree turn. The doors are open. Caden hops in. He helps Langley get on. It's my turn. Caden holds out his hand for me.

I hesitate.

"Kestrel?"

I look down at the hand that is reaching for mine. I see five fingers and five fingernails. His fingers are long and thin. That must help when he plays the guitar. I see three freckles on his hand, all very close together like good friends. I glance up. I am *in* the gondola! It worked! *Thanks, Breck.*

The car sways a little. *This isn't too bad.*

Inside the ice cube of death, there's one padded bench in front that faces the back and one in the back that faces front. There's enough room for three people on each bench—four if everyone scrunches. My knees are a bit noodly, so it's a relief to fall on the back bench next to my best friend. I look out the big pane of glass next to me, wondering how many more people will cram in with us. We are still moving, but no one else is getting on. It's a miracle! They are letting us go by ourselves!

A second before the doors close we hear a girl scream, "Caden, I love yoooooou!"

The car glides through the roundhouse. Once we leave the station, Caden collapses against the seat. "We made it!"

"That was close," says Langley.

I can't believe it. I'm here. I'm ON the gondola! As our ice cube glides upward, it makes no sound. I expected something—a creaking cable or the groan of metal—but there is only a slight whistle as air slips in through the vents above us. From the hundreds of fir trees in the distance, I pick out one. Just one. I keep my eyes on that tree. Once we pass it, I look for another tree. I do not look behind me at the valley or down at the ground or up at the sky. I look only at my tree. Out of the corner of my eye, I can see a support pole coming up to meet us. The car swings slightly as the cable rolls over the wheels connected to the top of the pole.

My breath catches. My heart skips one beat. Then two. I dig my fingernails into the cushion. This was a bad idea. What was I thinking? I can't do this. I am not ready for this. I am going to freak out in front of my best friend and the most popular teen rock star in the world! I feel funny. Light-headed. Tingly. Dizzy. I close my eyes. Oh, no! I am losing control. Something bad is about to happen. I know it. I *know* it! I wait for my throat to close off. I wait for my brain to shut down. I wait for my heart to explode out of my chest. I wait to die.

It sure is a long wait. I am still waiting when I hear a grunt. Wyatt's grunt.

Are you saying fear can't kill you? It just makes you think it can?

Bingo!

My breath is ragged, but I *am* still breathing. My throat isn't closing off. My thoughts are jumbled, but I *am* still thinking. My brain isn't shutting down. My heart is still in my chest and beating, if erratically. It isn't speeding up, though. It's slowing down. As panic eases its grip on me, I release my seat cushion. I inhale to the count of five. Then I exhale to the count of five, turning slightly to let the sun warm my face and shoulders. Slow breath in. Slow breath out. Soon, feeling begins to return to my extremities. I wait a few minutes more before opening my eyes. We are still moving up the slope toward a rocky crest. Even though it's scary not knowing what is on the other side of the ridge, I know I'll be all right. I'm not going to die.

Langley and Caden are watching me, worried.

"You all right?" asks Caden.

"I think so."

"I don't blame you for being jittery," he says. "We *are* pretty far off the ground." He glances around. "And this car is so . . . small."

It makes me feel better to know someone else isn't so comfortable either.

"Lang?" I tap her arm. "How did you find out I was scared of heights?"

"You're kidding, right?" She raises an eyebrow. "Kestrel, we've been best friends since the fifth grade. You don't think I notice that every time we go up the stairs you avoid the rail side? Or that you hardly ever want to go up to the second floor at the mall even though your favorite T-shirt shop is there? Or that whenever we go to the fair you make up some lame excuse so you won't have to go on the high rides?"

"I do?"

"Last year, you said you couldn't go on the roller coaster because you had a condition where your eardrums explode if the ride goes faster than ten miles per hour. The year before that you were allergic to the faux-leather seats. I'm not sure about the year before that, but I think it had something to do with a nosebleed—"

"Okay, okay. So why didn't you ever say something?"

She lifts a shoulder. "What was I supposed to say? Besides, I knew you'd work it out."

I sit back. How about that? All along I thought I was hiding my deepest, darkest Don't from the world, and Langley knew. She knew the whole time.

We continue our journey, and little by little, I lower my eyes. I see mountain bikers swerving down the dirt trails, leaving clouds of dust behind them. I see a line of hikers crossing the white, flat rocks in a glittering stream. I see a red-tailed hawk preening her mottled feathers on a pine branch. I am seeing the world from a completely different angle, one that is new and extraordinary and incredible.

And then it happens.

The gondola stops.

~ 16 ~
Don't Stand Up in a Gondola

aden is staring at me. Langley, too.

I raise my hands. "I didn't touch anything."

"It'll start up in a couple of minutes," says Langley. "I mean, they can't leave us hanging here." Her voice is getting smaller with each word. "Can they?"

It's too far between cars to clearly see the people in the cubes in front of or behind us, but I *can* see into one of the cars heading in the opposite direction. We passed them a few seconds before the gondola stopped, so we're only about thirty feet apart. They are suspended on a separate cable below ours. A little girl about five years old is sitting on her knees on the back bench. She has curly, carrot-red pigtails and is wearing a lavender dress and white tights. Her hands are spread out on the glass. She squints up at me. I grin and wave. She does the same. She doesn't seem scared.

We hear a crackle. It's coming from a speaker in the corner above me. "Ladies and gentlemen," says a male voice, "we apologize for the delay. We're taking care of a small maintenance issue. We should have it ironed out shortly and have you on your way soon. Thank you for your patience."

"As if we have a choice," mumbles Caden.

"There we go," says Langley. "I knew they wouldn't forget us."

"Bugs under glass," says Caden, wiping his brow. He's sitting in the sun. "Something's wrong."

"I'm sure everything's fine," I say. "They probably have to oil something or take a car out of service."

"Maybe Caden's right." Langley's forehead is against the glass as she looks down at the trail one hundred feet below us.

"Didn't you hear?" I ask. "He said it was a small maintenance issue—"

"Didn't *you* hear?" she shoots back. "He said they'd have it *ironed out soon*. You don't iron out a maintenance issue. You iron out a problem."

"I think we may have a problem of our own." I tip my head toward Caden, who is clutching his bench cushion so hard his knuckles are white. His head is tipped back against the window. Sweat glistens on his forehead.

"Uh-oh," says my best friend. "Caden, are you okay?"

"You bet. Sure. Great," he says, even as his eyes glaze over.

I know that look. Quickly, I pull my arms out of my hoodie. Bunching my jacket into a ball, I lean over and tuck it into the corner of his bench. "You've got a big concert to do, so why don't you rest a bit?"

"I don't know . . . I'm not sure . . . ," he sputters, but I am already taking him by the shoulders and gently easing him down so his head is on my makeshift pillow. There isn't enough room for him to completely stretch out. He has to bend his knees, but at least he's out of direct sunlight. I lift off his cap, which can only be making him hotter in this miniature greenhouse. I take the wig off too, and a wave of light blond hair tumbles out.

He puts a hand to his damp forehead. "Kestrel, I'm fine—"

"Close your eyes," I say.

He obeys.

"We're all going to take a minute and relax, okay?" I ease myself back down into my seat across from him. I glance at Langley. "Let's inhale to the count of five. Ready? One . . . two . . . three . . . four . . . five."

They both follow my instructions.

"Good. Now exhale as I count backward," I say, counting back from five down to zero. "Let's do it again. Slow breath in. Slow breath out. Perfect."

Caden flutters his eyelids.

"Keep them closed," I say. "Keep breathing. Let your mind help you gain control over your body. You're doing fine." I tap Langley on the knee. "Open the other vent," I whisper. "Text your mom and tell her we're stuck for a bit hanging out in the gondola but we're all okay. Say it like that, all right? I don't want anybody spreading any gossip about Caden."

"Okay," says Langley.

I turn back to my nervous pop star. "How are you feeling?"

"Like I got off a roller coaster going two hundred miles per hour."

"That's great. That you're off it, I mean."

"Sorry," he says. "I've never liked small, confined spaces, especially when those spaces aren't going anywhere. Sorry."

"There's nothing to be sorry for. Believe me. I know." I look out the window at the car suspended below us. The little girl in lavender is clutching her mother's leg. She doesn't look as happy as she did before. She is looking at me, so I make a silly face—crossing my eyes and sticking out my tongue. Then I pretend I am underwater, puffing out my cheeks and pretending to swim. I fake bumping my head on the glass. Lavender girl is grinning again.

Langley is busy texting. I remember how talking to my mom helped *me* when we were going over the Port Mann Bridge, so maybe it could help Caden, too. I should say something. I say the first thing that pops into my head. "Hey, uh . . . I could recite my poem for you—the one that won the contest, I mean, if you want to hear it."

"Uh-huh," he says.

I clear my throat and begin:

"You're sure I have things figured out. Know
who I am. What I want. Why I'm here.
I don't.
I'm sure you have things figured out. Know who
you are. What you want. Why you're here.
You don't.
Maybe you could admit, like me, you're a little lost.
Crisscrossed. Wind-tossed.
And maybe I could admit, like you, I'm a little scared.
Unprepared. Undeclared.
So let's not pretend we know anything
about who we are, what we want, and why
we're here.
Let's help each other live."

Caden opens his eyes. "That was good, Kestrel."

I dip my head shyly. "Nah."

"Told ya," said Langley.

"You look a lot better," I say to Caden, partly because it's true and partly to change the subject.

"Thanks. I'm feeling better. Guess I popped your rock-star bubble big-time, huh?"

"No," I say. "Nobody expects perfection."

His snort says I am wrong.

"It must be hard being famous," I say. "I mean, you think it would be cool to have everyone know you, but would it? After watching those wild girls back there, I'm not so sure."

"Don't you ever want to go to the store in your sweats and buy some jalapeño chips or something without photographers chasing you?" asks Langley.

"If only they chased me that wouldn't be so bad," says Caden. "But they do much worse. They make up things. Before you know it, you're on the cover of a magazine with the headline, 'Pop Star Out of Control: Is in Rehab for Jalapeño Addiction.'"

Langley and I laugh, as he meant for us to, but Caden's grin is pained.

"People think fame makes you bigger," he says. "It does the opposite. It shrinks your world. You can't go anywhere or do anything. You end up hiding out. Even *after* I leave a place, it's mobbed. People want to stay in the room I stayed in or steal the towel I touched. At my last hotel, fans broke into my room and searched for hair and fingernail clippings. It's totally weird."

"Ew," I say, but Langley has a *What's wrong with that?* expression on her face.

"I try to stick with my old friends, the ones I knew before I became famous, you know, but even then you can't always trust them." He turns to me. "Kestrel, are you gonna tell—?"

"No," I say firmly. "We're not ever going to say anything to anybody about this lift trip, are we, Langley?"

"Absolutely not. What happens in the gondola stays in the gondola."

"Thanks," he says. "Funny how things work out. I sure am glad of that leak now."

I tip my head. "Leak?"

"I was supposed to stay at the Fairmont, but someone let it slip, so we ended up diverting to your lodge," he says. "You guys were the only ones with enough rooms for all of us on such short notice. Plus, you're off the beaten track, so—"

"That's it!" I leap up, sending the car swaying. "Sorry, sorry!" I plunk my butt back down. "I thought of something we could do to help business at the lodge."

Langley eyes are wide. "What?"

"Caden says people flock to any place he stays, right? We'll leak it to the media that he stayed at our lodge—"

"And the reservations will come pouring in," finishes Langley. "It's brilliant!"

I turn to Caden. "We won't tell anyone until after you've checked out, I swear."

"If it'll help business, I'd be happy to mention I stayed there," he says. "I can tell a few friends about it too."

"That would be amazing." With Caden's help we could fill the lodge twice as fast!

We feel a sudden lurch.

"We're moving!" cries Caden.

Langley and I cheer! As we sail upward, I glance down to the gondola going the opposite way. The little girl in lavender is wiggling her fingers. I wave back.

Caden's concert is . . .

Beyond stellar. It is phenomenal. It is incredible. It is every positive adjective that exists or will ever exist in the entire universe. Langley and I dance in the aisles. We take dozens of videos and photos. We sing along to every song, and I almost spontaneously combust when Caden brings us up onstage—*yes, up onstage*—to sing "Hangin' by a Thread."

"Still hanging by a thread from your heart." Langley sings the first line with him.

I take the second line. "You kept me on a string from the start."

We sing the last lines together. "If only you would untie the knot, we could both be free. We could both be free."

Caden does a two-hour concert inside the theater for the three hundred or so guests at the party. While onstage,

I spot Veranda and Rose in the second row on the opposite side of the auditorium. Her arms folded in front of her, Veranda seems to be pouting. I bet she wanted to go up onstage too. Caden is singing his final notes of the encore song. I put my arm around my best friend. "I'm so glad I got on the gondola with you," I shout.

"What?"

"I said I'm so glad I came up the mountain."

"What?"

"Are your ears still ringing? We're close to the amps."

"My ears are ringing. We're too close to the amps."

It's over. Everyone claps and yells until our hands are sore and our throats are raw. Langley and I file out of the theater with the rest of the guests. I turn at the steps, leading us up to the observation deck and through the outdoor café.

"Before we go back down, let's take a picture by the Inukshuk," I say as we wind our way through the tables.

"The what-shack?"

"The Inukshuk." I point to tall sculpture in the shape of a human made from five stacked stones. "I read about it in one of the brochures at the lodge. They were created by ancient Inuits to mark navigational routes. This one was built for the 2010 Olympics."

We pick our way down a steep slope to reach the sculpture at the edge of a rocky cliff. It's more than double my height and stands on a cement platform, facing the valley. It's a long way down to the village below—1,850 meters, which sets the hair on my arms at attention. I'm wary, but not worried.

Standing shoulder to shoulder, Langley and I look at the view. From this height, Whistler village looks like a toy model, even the big hotels seem tiny. The blue-and-white mountains stretch forever. Here and there, the tallest rocky peaks pierce bloated silver clouds. The tree-lined hills rising up from the valley floor remind of how Langley's cat, Mouse, looks when he's hiding under a blanket.

"You can see the whole valley from here," says Langley. "Look, there's the Fairmont."

My eye lands on the large rectangle building that's bent at both ends then moves right to the swatches of green carved into the base of the hillside. "There's the golf course," I say.

"And Lost Lake," says Langley, and our eyes pan down to the sapphire bunny-shaped lake below the golf course.

I scan the trees. "Where's the lodge?"

"There!"

"Where?" I see the bigger condos, the Four Seasons, and the Alpenglow, but no Blackcomb Creek Lodge.

"Go diagonally up the hill from the lake."

"I don't see it."

"You can see the very top of the roof sticking up past the big bump in the hill. Did you start at the lake?"

"I did, but I still don't see it."

"For goodness' sake, Kestrel, if all those itty-bitty toads can find their way—"

"Got it." In my defense, most of the lodge is hidden by a wrinkle in the hill. From here, I can barely make out the top of the A-line roof. "I thought it would be farther up the mountain—"

Itty-bitty toads?

Of course! Why didn't I see it sooner? Maybe I was too

close. From here, from the top of the world, everything is clear. It makes perfect sense!

"Kestrel?" Langley's hand is in front of my face. "Is it your height thing again? Maybe we should go down—"

"I know what to do, Langley," I say as the wind animates my hair. "I know how to save the lodge from the Terrible Tollivers."

17

Dare to Make a Difference— No Matter How Small

"Toads?" Grandma Lark's brow furrows. "Toads are going to keep the lodge afloat?"

"Hear me out," says Dr. Musgraves, unrolling a map. Mom, Dad, and I help him flatten it out on the table. We are in the dining room. It's the middle of the afternoon, so we have the place to ourselves. "Here's Lost Lake, and here"—the professor's finger travels several inches to the northeast—"is your acreage, Lark. It sits directly in the migration path of *Bufo boreas*."

"That's the western toad," I say.

"Yes, I know," says my grandmother. "The little hoppers have been crossing our property for as long as I've lived here, but Jerome, I still don't see how—"

"Over the years, each of these larger properties around you has been sold to developers." Dr. Musgraves takes out a pen. "See? Here's the Alpenglow and the Four Seasons and one, two, three, four condos." He crosses out the sections of land that have been built on. "You own quite a bit of acreage, Lark. Yours is one of only two remaining parcels that gives the toads a direct migratory route from the lake up the mountain. And the data my students and I have collected, so far, shows a significant percentage of the migrating toads from Lost Lake are following the creek bed and crossing your property."

"How significant?" asks my grandmother.

"It's still early in the season, but preliminary data is showing thirty-two percent."

My mom gasps. "That many?"

"It could go much higher by the end of the season," says Dr. Musgraves. "Perhaps, to fifteen or even twenty thousand toads."

"That's more than half the population!" I say.

Grandma Lark's green eyes grow. "So you're saying . . ."

"Your land is vital to the survival of this toad population," says Dr. Musgraves. "When Kestrel brought it to my attention that you were considering selling, I contacted the fisheries conservation group I work with. The director says he's interested in spearheading a plan to purchase a substantial piece of your land for amphibian preservation. The land could never be built on, which means the remaining section of your property, here where the lodge sits, would hardly be attractive to a developer. It's not a large enough for a condo or hotel complex."

"Western toads are blue-listed," says Dad, "so even if a builder *was* interested, they'd have to conduct exhaustive and expensive environmental impact studies and go through a lengthy series of hearings to get approval. Trust me, Mom, I can tie them up in court for most of Kestrel's life, if necessary. If the Tollivers know what's good for them, they won't want anything to do with our property once the conservation group gets involved."

"And the money from the sale of the property should help you with the necessary repairs to this place," says Mom.

My grandmother puts a hand to her cheek. "You mean—"

"You won't lose the lodge, Grandma," I say.

My grandmother slowly sinks into a chair. "I don't know what to say." Her eyes tearing, she looks around our little circle, from Dad to Mom to me to Dr. Musgraves. "Thank you."

"There's something else, Mom," says my dad. "We want to help you financially until business bounces back."

"No, I couldn't—"

"Yes, you could. Norah, Kestrel, Wyatt, and I talked it over, and it's settled. We're family, and this lodge means as much to us as it does to you. I should have said so sooner." Dad smiles at me. "Besides, something tells me business is going to pick up soon."

"I think it already has." Mom is standing next to the window. "Look!"

Everyone rushes over. There must be at least five hundred people in the parking lot—most of them under the age of eighteen and most of them girls! They are pointing their phones at the windows, front door, and balconies, hoping for a glimpse of Caden Christopher. They won't get it. He left early this morning, exactly thirty seconds after giving Dinah permission to let the cat out of the bag.

I look down at the full parking lot. *Thanks, Caden.*

"It's a hot day out there," says Grandma Lark, heading for the kitchen. "We'd better break out the lemonade."

I hurry after her. "Let's give them Lemon Fizz soda. We've got a whole fridge full of the stuff."

In shorts and tees, Langley and I stroll past the line of people waiting for Dinah and Aubrey to check them in. Aubrey Farraday is Jess's replacement. She's a few years older than Dinah, but just as cute, with dozens of freckles on her nose and cheeks, and naturally curly hair the color of caramel. Aubrey is smart and friendly, but I think we are all a little scared to completely trust anyone new. It will take time.

Outside, I stop on the flagstone to retie my tennis shoes.

This is Langley's and my last run together. She and her mom are going home tomorrow. Mrs. Derringer has to get back to work. I hoped Langley would stay for the rest of the summer, but she has to get back too. She's got piano lessons and tennis lessons, and she misses her cat, Mouse. I think she misses Aaron, too. I know she planned on accidentally running into him at the lake at least twice this summer.

We jog the trail to Lost Lake and stop at the amphibian fence so Langley can see the toads one last time. There aren't quite as many as last week. They are bunched up in groups on the sand, warming themselves in the late-afternoon sun. As we walk the length of the fence, they hear our vibrations and hop into the beach grass. We follow the shoreline up to the path so we can stop at the toad underpass.

"Careful," I say to a woman in neon yellow shorts jogging toward us. "There are toads crossing here."

She pulls up. "Where?"

"There's one about two inches in front of your foot."

She squeals. "That's a toad? Oh, my gosh, I didn't even see him. Thanks for telling me." She forgets all about her jog and spends the next ten minutes inching along behind her toad until he makes it safely to the other side. I know the feeling. There is something about these fragile, bumpy, clumsy creatures that touches you. You can't help but want to protect them.

"Excellent work, Kestrel Adams, amphibian protector," Langley says in her best news announcer voice. "Another day, another toad saved."

"And same to you, Langley Derringer, trusty toad assistant."

At the footbridge, Langley gets on her knees to peer under the planks. "They're still coming through."

I kneel next to her. A group of little brown heads are bobbing toward us. The toad traffic jam isn't as heavy as last time, yet it's still busy. I'd say a six on a scale of one to ten.

I have not forgotten Dr. Musgraves's warning that only 1 percent of the toads will ever return. Still, I'd like to think that all of the hard work everyone has done—the fence, the netting, the underpass, the signs—means many of the toads that would not have survived will make it back next March to lay their eggs. And who knows? Once the conservation group buys Grandma's land, maybe one day this site could be home to the biggest western toad population in the world. Wouldn't that be something?

"Bye, toads," says Langley.

"Bye, toads," I echo. "See your kids next summer."

18
Don't Forget to Remember

I am sitting on the deck of our suite, the chair tipped back as far as it can go, with my neck tipped back as far as *it* can go. The sky is a deep indigo. Only a sliver of moon hovers above the rounded black silhouette of the hill. Thousands of stars are winking, as if competing for my attention in some kind of celestial beauty pageant. I see Vega in the east. That's the only star I can remember by name. Music floats up from the patio, just around the corner. Someone is playing an acoustic guitar. I don't know the song, but it has a Spanish feel to it. People laugh. Glasses clink.

I close my eyes the way a camera closes its shutter and take a picture with my mind. *Click.* I have been doing that all week. Everywhere I go in the lodge, I spend a few minutes committing things to memory so I won't forget them when we go home in a few days. The elegant cream-and-blue dining room, where the chairs and napkins match and on every clear summer night, the room is painted pink by the setting sun. *Click.* The little library with its hollowed-out shelves and red-and-green plaid chairs and lamp with the stained-glass frogs chasing each other around the shade. Dinah and Aubrey at the front desk handing out maps and key cards and advice to the tourists. Breck, George, and Kyle rolling their squeaky luggage carts through the lobby. *Click.* *Click. Click.* I have been taking photos with my phone, too, but there are some things that can only be captured by your heart. I don't want to ever forget how close we came to losing Blackcomb Creek Lodge.

I slap away a mosquito. I guess I'd better go in. I'll sure miss seeing the stars when we go home, which is kind of funny when you think about it. They are the very same stars

I can see at home, but how different they are here.

Going in, I lock the door behind me. "Mom, can I walk around inside for a bit?"

Her eyes shift from her book to her watch.

"I know it's after ten," I say, "but I'm not tired. And Wyatt isn't back yet."

"Got your phone?"

I pat the back pocket of my jeans.

Leaving our suite, I walk down the hall to the elevator. Instead of pressing the button, I step into the little nook that overlooks the lobby the way I did the first day we got here. The scent of warm, buttered popcorn wafts up from below. It's movie night in the dining room. Wyatt is there with Grandma Lark. They should be getting out soon.

I lean my elbows on the rail and look down. The lobby is empty, except for Aubrey behind the desk. She is sorting papers, placing them into four neat stacks.

Ding!

The elevator opens. Breck steps off. He's carrying a paper shopping bag. "Everything okay?"

"Uh-huh."

"Fly on the wall, eh?" He holds up the bag. "I'd ask you to come along, but we know how dangerous that can be."

I break out in a full-blown case of lobsteritis. In the few minutes it takes for my face to return to its normal shade, Breck is back.

"Hey, you're makin' progress," he says.

"Huh?"

"You're *leaning* on the rail."

He's right. I am!

"I hadn't thought about it," I say

"That's the idea." Breck comes to lean beside me. There is barely enough room in the nook for the two of us. "My shift is done," he says, surveying the lobby. "I'm waiting for my mom to finish up in the kitchen."

"I'm . . . uh . . . waiting for Wyatt to get out of the movie."

Our elbows are touching. Breck's left hand is holding his right elbow. My right hand is holding my left elbow.

"Movie should be over soon," he says.

"Soon," I say, letting my gaze drop to the first floor. I'm

almost daring myself to get jittery or dizzy or sick to my stomach, but nothing happens.

"Leaving on Saturday, huh?" he asks.

"Yeah, but we'll be back for Christmas."

"Sounds like we'll still be here."

"Grandma says the lodge is almost fully booked for the winter."

"That's great news."

"It turned out to be a good summer, after all, didn't it?"

"It sure did." Breck's index finger taps mine. He curls it around my knuckle. I bend my finger and we are linked together. Together, we watch the comings and goings below. Aubrey is humming while she straightens her stacks. A young mother has taken a seat in one of the overstuffed chairs next to the fireplace and is feeding her baby a bottle of formula. An elderly couple strolls, hand in hand, toward the library. I could stay here forever, leaning over the rail next to Breck, seeing a world that can't see us. Yep. Forever. If only my brother weren't charging up the stairs, yelling, "Kes, you missed some wicked dinosaurs!"

Click.

19

Dare to Do One Thing Every Day That Scares You

The fiery orange sun dips toward the whipped meringue mountaintops. The cloudless sky is easily changing colors, from daytime's rich topaz to evening's deep delphinium blue. A brisk breeze wraps my hair around my neck and sends goose bumps down my arms. I am at the top of Blackcomb Peak with my grandmother. It's my first time here. I had to ride a lift where you sit in a chair with a clear dome over your head and your legs dangle freely. Yes, *dangle*! Argggh! I won't lie. I *was* scared, but I knew I could do it.

I know my grandmother was afraid to come up too. Not

because of the chairlift but because the last time she was here was with Grandpa Keith. They watched the sunset together, the way we are watching it now. Out of the corner of my eye, I sneak glances at her profile. I stay alert for anything that might indicate the memories are too much for her. The wind is whisking her short white hair into spikes. I see sorrow in her eyes, but no pain. Hugging my jean jacket closer, I look down the mountain. I can see our lodge. *Our* lodge.

"I'm going to miss you," says Grandma Lark.

"Me, too," I say. We are going home tomorrow. "The summer went by so fast."

It's strange to hear myself so that. I practically dropped dead when my mother told the border officer we were going to stay a month or two. Now it's a foggy memory, as if it happened ages and ages ago and to somebody else. I can't imagine spending my summer anywhere but here.

"It's getting chilly," says Grandma Lark, closing the zipper of her white Windbreaker. "Ready to go?"

"Can we wait a few more minutes? For the green flash? Tell me what to do."

"You sound like your grandfather," she says, then turns me slightly so we are facing the sun straight on. "Focus on the horizon. Look at the *top* of the sun, right before it disappears."

We stay as still as an Inukshuk statue. I keep my eyes glued to where the peaks meet the sky. "Grandma?"

"Yes?"

"Do you think I could ever be as good as Dinah? You know, when it comes to hospitality?"

"I do," she says without hesitation. "It's in your blood."

It is, isn't it? This place and everything in it is part of me now. I belong here. I am a girl with her foot in two countries, and I am at home in both.

Only about a quarter of the sun is still visible. The orange orb is slipping behind the mountain range.

Going . . .

A curved slice.

Going . . .

The thinnest of stripes.

Going . . .

An emerald-green flare.

"There!" I shout.

Gone.

"Grandma Lark! The green flash? Did you see it?"

"I did," she cries. "I did!"

We grab each other and hold on as tight as we can. We keep gazing at the horizon, half expecting another miracle to occur, but nothing does. The sky is turning a deep purple, the silhouette of the mountain range fading from view.

"Time to go," says my grandmother, though she does not release me.

"Let's take the Peak 2 Peak gondola," I say.

"Across the valley? It's the long way."

"I know, but I've never been in a gondola with a see-through floor before." Hearing myself say it out loud makes me nervous. "On second thought, we don't have to. It *is* kind of scary."

My grandmother gives me a devilish grin. "Then we have no choice, Little Bird. We *must* go that way."

She's right, of course.

And so we do.

Acknowledgments

Special thanks to:

Alyson Heller, my talented editor, who helps me to be a better writer and person; Rosemary Stimola, my incredible agent, who is as kind as she is wise; my parents, for their faith and support; William, whose love makes all things possible; Lauren, Daniel, and the dedicated staff at Fairmont Gold at Fairmont Chateau Whistler; and Whistler, BC, whose breathtaking beauty inspired this book.